ADDICTED TO Sin 2:

A Taste of Sin

NEYARA

Published by Shani Greene-Dowdell Presents, Opelika, AL
www.nayberrypublications.com

To receive future updates from Shani Greene-Dowdell Presents, text Nayberry to 22828 or sign up at www.nayberrypublications.com

CHAPTER ONE

Sinaiyah

"Sin, you know that I still love you." Courtland spoke softly.

Courtland was standing in my doorway with the most sincere look on his face I had ever seen. It had been a while since I had last seen him, and I really missed him, I mean *really* missed him. Courtland was that one guy that I couldn't let go of, clearly. I called myself trying to detox off of him, by not speaking to him, and ridding myself of all thoughts of him, but it ended up having a reverse effect and made me miss him even more. I missed how he made me feel like a princess, and that I was worth loving. I missed being in his arms, and feeling safe whenever he was around. I just missed everything about him, and how he made me feel. I had to shake those emotions off of me, because in this moment, with Courtland standing in front of me, I had to keep a straight face, which was hard to do, especially with my level of alcohol intake.

"I don't think I'm ready to digest what you're saying on an emotional level, Courtland." I forced down another sip from the bottle of whiskey I was holding. My stomach was turning, and I knew I had better stopped, because my body couldn't handle any more. Courtland tried to walk past me, but I blocked him from coming any further into my condo.

"I can understand that." He took a step back into the hallway. "Would you like to grab some lunch in the city with me?"

"Stop." I placed my hand in front of his face. "Just stop. I have told you over and over, no. I don't want to go to the city with you. I live in the city. I don't need you to go anywhere with me." I could feel my blood running hot through my body.

"I understand that, but I would like to sit down with you and talk." He remained calm.

I shifted my weight from one leg to the other. "So why do you want to go to the city now?" I was interested in what he had to say.

Courtland had been trying to get me to leave my condo for at least two months now, and my answer had been and still was no. I wasn't sure if I was ready to see crowds of people. I had become accustomed to my life of solidarity, and I needed him to respect that.

"You haven't been around people in three months, hell you haven't even been around me."

"Maybe I don't like people," I folded my arms across my chest, "maybe I don't like you." I replied in a matter of fact tone.

I took a deep breath and looked down at my bare feet. I could have really used a pedicure right now. Truthfully, I was longing to get out of the house and enjoy the world I once couldn't get enough of. Courtland caressed my arms. I could tell he knew that I wanted out of my newfound isolated world. I looked up at his handsome face and could see that he felt bad for me with his soft eyes, clenched lip, and creased forehead. A piece of me wanted to hate him, because he was partially the reason why my life had been stripped from me, but I felt like I couldn't blame him for everything that went down at Perceptions last year.

"I promise you, all I want to do is protect you." Courtland words interrupted my thoughts. His eyes still seemed sincere, which made me smile shyly at him. I quickly looked away from him, and placed my hand on the door. I wasn't ready to trust him, at least not right now.

"Uh-huh, I know." I was about to take another swig, but Courtland grabbed the bottle from me.

"Sin, I'm worried about you."

"Oh, so now you worry." I placed my hand on my hips, "You weren't worried when my ass was handed to your momma. You weren't worried when you knew the feds were about to bust into Perceptions. You weren't worried when I lost our baby." I was furious with him now, and I wasn't done yet. I had so much anger built up inside of me, that I was ready to explode. "But I took one little sip of whiskey, and you're worried. Know that

3

when I say this, it's coming from the bottom of my heart, fuck you, Courtland!"

I slammed the door in his face, forcing him to leave. I didn't want to see him anymore.

I was ready for the Lord to take me. I had nothing to live for. I was ready to go to Heaven, if it still existed. I couldn't help myself from crying. I was so hurt. I grabbed the glass vase filled with white roses from my decorative table in the hallway and slammed it against the wall, watching as the glass shattered and roses fall near my feet.

I leaned against the wall adjacent to the door and squatted. I had to be crazy to still love this man, but I did. I cradled myself on the floor, and cried harder. I was mentally drained and an emotional mess.

Through tear filled eyes, I saw my front door swing open. Courtland slowly stepped inside. He closed the door behind him, and looked down at me. I couldn't move. I didn't want him to see me like this, but I had to let my pride go. Deep down, I appreciated him for being around. I was no longer sure if I could trust the woman I was becoming.

"Let's go grab lunch." Courtland spoke with a pained expression on his face. He bended down on one knee, and ran his hand through my tangled hair that I hadn't really comb in days. He wiped the tears from my eyes and picked me up.

Stepping over the broken glass and roses on the floor, he took me to my bedroom to get me dressed.

Watching him maneuver my dresser drawers and find an outfit almost made me cry. These were the moments I missed the most. He took his time getting me dressed in a little black sundress. He buckled my sandals, and remembered to grab a pair of earrings and my watch that I never left home without.

He left out of the room, and I stood up from my bed and walked over to my vanity, and brushed my hair up into a bun. It had been a long time since I had seen myself look like a lady. I could hear him sweeping up the glass from the floor. I felt bad for myself, I had been living in misery and the one person who I wanted to save me was coming to my rescue, and I didn't know how to accept it; even though it was what my heart desired.

Courtland came back into my bedroom, and reached his hand out to me. I grabbed his hand and stood up from my spot on the bed. He walked me to the door, and I quickly grabbed the liquor bottle on our way out. I didn't want any of it to go to waste. Watching Courtland lock the door with his key reminded me that I hadn't changed the locks on the doors like always threatened to him I would. I wanted to keep him out, but deep down I felt like I needed him to come and check on me from time to time.

I sat silently in my comfy halter sundress, wearing my all black sunglasses as we rode outside the city. After being confined for so long, seeing people was weird, and I felt like an outsider.

Twenty minutes later we parked on the street in front of some little sugar shack that was overflowing with people.

"I don't want to eat here," I whispered to Courtland. He looked over at me with a huge smile as he turned off the car. Seeing this many people in one spot was making me nervous, but I knew he wouldn't understand where I was coming from.

"It's going to be okay. I got you." He jumped out of his side of the truck, and came around to open my door.

"Yeah, because I have so much trust in you." I couldn't help my sarcasm, even though I had more trust in him than I was willing to openly acknowledge.

He reached for my hand, and I politely motioned to him that I had it. I got out of my car like a real woman, even as I missed my step, and stumbled out of the car. I may have looked foolish, but I hopped up to my feet quickly. I needed to get it together quick.

"Tell her to seat us outside," I said, pointing to the hostess without making any eye contact with her. As he walked away, I held my purse tightly, and leaned against the truck to watch my surroundings. I felt so uncomfortable, out of my element. I wanted to be on my sofa, listening to Adele, with a drink in my left hand and another one in my right.

"Right this way," I heard the hostess say.

Courtland came back towards me, grabbed my hand, and pulled me behind him. I stayed close, holding my purse even tighter. I didn't have anything in it but a bottle of Hennessey, but it was mine, and no one else's. I felt like I had to protect it. It seemed like everyone was watching me.

"Your waitress will be here momentarily." The hostess was a pleasant looking college girl with a cheerful smile. *Oh, what I wouldn't give to be young and free again.*

I sat down, but didn't feel safe. I had this crazy feeling that someone would recognize me and humiliate me. I couldn't deal with anymore public humiliation. The entire time the Perceptions scandal went on I was humiliated. I couldn't go down the street without someone recognizing me, and asking me questions they knew I couldn't answer. I would walk past women and be called a whore, or a home-wrecker, or they would shame me with other hurtful words. I was constantly looking over my shoulder. I didn't trust anyone.

"Why would you bring me to the most crowded place in town? I would have much preferred the drive-thru at McDonalds, or Zaxby's," I whispered to him, with my irritation showing all over my face.

"Calm down, Sin." He chuckled a little.

I turned my coffee mug up, and poured myself a cup full of Hennessey.

"You is so smart." I was talking to myself, as I lifted my coffee mug, and blew it like it was coffee. "Looks like coffee, but is good ole Hennessey." I raised it to him, and took a big gulp.

"Sin, you gotta calm down with all the drinking."

"Why?" I held my purse tighter. "I try not to mix my lights and my darks." I had learned that lesson the hard way a couple of times early on in my isolation.

"All the liquor you drink can't be healthy, babe." He had a smile on his face, but I knew he was serious.

"It may not be healthy, but it's much needed. That's why God has sent someone to supply me with new bottles on a weekly basis." I winked at him, and drank some more.

He shook his head in disapproval.

"You see anything on the menu you want?"

"I can't read." I pushed my sunglasses up on my nose, and I could feel the top of my nose starting to sweat.

"Really, Sin?"

"I don't want to be here," I told him, as I looked from side to side. "I'm only here because you brought me."

I hadn't been around a crowd of people in three months. I alienated myself from the world to stay out of the public's eye, so being out felt like torture.

"Well, you have to eat something. With all the drinking you've been doing lately, you need something else in your stomach."

"You're right." I leaned back in my seat. "I was starting to miss wine too. Let's be sure to grab some before we head back."

"Something other than liquor, Sin! You have to eat."

"Get me a piece of salmon." I tilted my head down and looked at him over my shades, as if I were James Bond. "Blackened."

He chuckled. I liked seeing him laugh. We had been through hell, so to see him laugh made me feel really good.

Our food came out and I took my time eating. I couldn't remember when I had eaten a complete meal. Sitting there, it finally hit me: I am a sad case, especially since I had forced myself to survive off of liquor, and I had no intention of changing my bad habits.

We made it back home before dark, and I was happy to have four new bottles of wine. Thanks to Courtland, I now had two bottles of white and two bottles of red. I did restock on my ole faithfuls too. With this much stock, it should last me for at least a week.

I opened one bottle of white wine. I grabbed a glass and filled it all the way to the top. I danced around in a circle happy to have something sweet. I swayed from side-to-side to a tune that I couldn't stop hearing in my mind.

I was happy that Courtland had gotten me out of the house. It felt good to step out into the world, but my mind couldn't help but wander.

One hundred and eighteen days.

That's how long I had been in hiding.

That's how long I had been emotionally devastated.

That's how long I had been waiting.

I was waiting for my sanity and for my life that I had once known to return, but most importantly I was waiting for Victoria and that bitch Illeanna. Waiting for them to receive the ass whooping they both so desperately deserved.

For the past six months, I had been in my condo scared for my damn life, because of their foolishness.

I still couldn't believe Illeanna had backstabbed me the way she had. Viviana had to sit me down like I was a child in church and tell me why I shouldn't try and help Illeanna, or bail her out. I was such a fool, accepting all her calls from jail, and sending her money when she was trying to get me locked up too. Judge Hill caught that messy shit too. Thank God for having a good judge that understood my "real" role in this mess.

That messy trial only lasted three months for me. The judge quickly threw my name out after reviewing all of the facts. Thank God she did. I just knew she was going to make a lesson out of me. I guess some Black women could hold power without belittling other Black women. After that mercy she showed me, I refused to get in any trouble. I stayed in the house. Thanks to Jaslynn, my alcohol supply and fridge were stocked once a week. Although it really didn't matter, because I was losing weight and depressed.

On the bright side, I had taken up new hobbies. I did puzzles, read a few novels, and even did a few latch-hook kits, but what I loved to do the most was drink. I drank no less than six glasses of anything a day, Sunday through Saturday.

I knew I had lost my mind when I called home and cried to my mom, asking her to come stay with me. Throughout the entire trial she tried to come, but I managed to keep her away. I didn't want her or my father anywhere in the press; it was my nightmare, not theirs. I was tired of being alone now, and I needed to be around somebody that knew me and loved me. Surprisingly enough, I wouldn't be alone for long because Lanette Lockhart was on her way.

I was trying not to let this crumble me. Because I didn't lose my esthetician license during the trial, Jaslynn encouraged me to start my own company. I didn't have anybody else, so I did appreciate her motivation and friendship. She had so much faith in me. It took me about a month to think of a name and my business outline, but once I put it together Jaslynn took off with it. She was heaven sent. She had completed the paperwork to start my company, put my website together, and started planning a grand opening brunch.

Courtland was around, but he tried to give me space, so I could go through this moment how I wanted to. The only times I spoke to him were when I was pissy drunk, and that was usually towards the end of the day.

He kept telling me that he wasn't going anywhere, and six months later, I was starting to believe him.

I stopped dancing, when I realized there was nothing in my glass. I went to the kitchen and stared out the window trying to figure my next move: Hennessey or Rum and Coke.

I could hear Courtland walking around my condo. I was ready to start feeling the alcohol a little more and I needed him to leave now. I didn't have time for him, and his rational self, when I had to make life decisions. My mother was on her way, and I wasn't sure if I was ready for her in my personal space as I much as I thought I was.

"Need any help?" he asked.

"Nope."

I decided to keep it simple; I chose the Whiskey. I needed one last shot.

"You excited about your grand opening?"

Hearing him talk about my business made me stop in my tracks. I turned around and gave him a confused look. He had me twisted if he thought I would discuss my business endeavors with him.

"What did I tell you about asking about my company?" I took a shot of whiskey.

"That was a basic question," he laughed in arrogance.

"Yea. I'm real excited." I poured myself another shot.

"I can tell," he said with a smirk.

"You can leave." I didn't have time to play with Courtland. I wanted another shot, but I decided against it.

"I understand that because of everything that happened, you have trust issues, but I don't understand why you're having such a hard time trusting me."

"Oh, I trust you." I placed the glass on the kitchen island. "I trust that you can find yourself out of my condo."

"Sin, don't be like that," he leaned over the kitchen island towards me.

"What have I told you to call me?"

He sucked in air as if he was upset. "Ms. Lockhart, don't be like that."

"Thank you." I said looking away from him. "Think you get special privileges and shit. Fuck no!" I was talking aloud although I was talking to myself. I needed to pee, I was drunk; there was no denying that. The fact that I was being extra was enough proof. "What you worried about?" I asked. I could see his worried look out the corner of my eye.

"I can't really say," he looked guilty.

"Oh!" I looked at him like the dummy he was. "Okay." Now, I needed another shot.

"Don't start," he hesitated.

"You're the one with secrets that are eating away at your soul." I tapped my polished nails against my granite counter top.

He shook his head in disapproval.

"How's Victoria?" I honestly didn't give a damn, but whatever was eating at him, I'm sure she was the root of it.

"They were looking for her," he answered.

I was surprised that he gave me a real answer.

"No shit, Sherlock! Hell, they asked me where her ass was."

"So then you know what happened."

"Fuck you, Courtland." I threw my hands up in the air, and headed to the front door. I was tired of him talking to me like I was a fool.

He swung me around by my arm, forcing me to face him. That made me a little dizzy, but I could hold my liquor so much better now. I looked out the window behind him, because I couldn't look him in his blueish-gray eyes. Although I hated him, I still had so much love for him. I just was not in love with him.

"You need to get it together, Sinaiyah."

"So you're telling me that they are no longer looking for Victoria." That's when the thought slipped into my mind, and happiness shot throughout my body. "Is she dead?" Curiosity was getting the best of me.

"Oh my God!" He took a deep breath and let go of me.

My doorbell rang, and I knew it was my mother.

I grabbed the bottle of whiskey and took a sip straight from the bottle.

"I'll be back!" I shouted, and stumbled to the front door.

My doorbell rang again, and I could hear my mother calling for me from outside. I walked to the door, took another sip of the whiskey, put the bottle down on the decorative table where my glass vase and white roses once stood and opened the door.

"Momma!" I threw my arms up to embrace her.

"Wait a minute." She held my arm and stopped me from hugging her. "Is that alcohol I smell on your breath?"

"I mean, momma…" I didn't want to have this discussion at the moment. "I had a sippy-sip her and there." I couldn't tell her that I found love in alcohol. Plus, it wasn't a big deal, and I didn't want her over exaggerating anything to daddy.

"No, you little liar, you had a bottle or more here and now. I can smell it through your pores." She pushed through the door and grabbed the whiskey bottle from the hallway table.

"Momma, not now." I was whining like a child.

"Oh, you're here?" she looked past me.

I turned around and saw Courtland standing in the entryway.

"Bring my bags in from the hallway and then leave." She motioned him towards the door.

"How are you feeling, baby?" She held my face in the palms of her hands and made me look directly into her eyes. I was trying to hold all of my emotions together, but I couldn't and I cried instantly.

"Let it out, my baby." My mother held me tightly, and rocked me back and forth.

I couldn't believe that I was finally letting go.

Who had I become? I thought I was content with the new life I had made for myself, but I wasn't. I just wanted my old life back. The peaceful, carefree life I enjoyed so much.

I was tired of holding in all of that pain. It hadn't been doing me any good anyway, so I was happy to finally be free, and let go.

CHAPTER TWO

Courtland

I had never seen Sin like that before. She was needy. Not annoying girlfriend needy, but daughter who needs a mother's love needy, and I was happy that she was getting that love. So much had happened over these past few months, and I was happy that she didn't hate me or hold any real resentment towards me.

It was heartbreaking to have to put all of the plans I had for us on hold. I hated not being able to show her everything I had started, and not being able to help her with her own endeavors was soul retching.

I left her place, and headed to work on some of my own projects. With everything that happened with Kensington and Company, I didn't want to bring any more attention to my own affairs. I lucked out and got off with community service. My lawyer did a damn good job in persuading the jury into believing that I was a glorified bodyguard, and the outcast in the family because I was the son Victoria didn't want. Victoria made it easy for the jury to believe my lawyer. She would walk in the courtroom like she owned with Jackson by her side the entire trial. I was left alone with a separate lawyer, and she would never look my way, or acknowledge me, even when she was asked to when she was on the stand. There were so many things that worked for me, especially with my last name not being Kensington. Jackson had it dealt to him being that he was the Director of Internal Affairs. He was looked at as the right hand man in everything that happened in the company, because everything had to go through him, or at least that's how it looked on paper.

The only time I did was for beating Donny's, or "Landon's" ass in the police station parking lot. I couldn't believe that he befriended me to get next to Sin. I didn't know that he knew her, and that they had a history. He did a great job of holding in his secret too. I could have killed him with my bare hands when I saw him grab Sin by the waist and kiss her like she was his woman. I didn't care what their history was; we were making our own history, and he was not a part of the plan.

"It's about time you got here!"

I pulled up at Viv's house. She had invited me over to have dinner with her and Damien, so that we could discuss what was next for me.

"I'm not sure why you feel the need to rush me." I rolled my windows up and got out of my truck.

"What? You had to do your community service this morning?" she laughed.

"Actually, yes, two more weeks and I'll be done." We both laughed and I gave her a hug.

"What are you doing outside anyway?" she was knee deep in soil.

"I have to check on my flowers. They didn't bloom, and I needed to check out some things.

"Oh, okay, is the front door open? Because I'm going inside." Yard work was not my thing.

"Shut-up and come on. I'm done anyway." She handed me a bucket full of tools, and she grabbed the open bag of soil.

"How's business?" I asked her. She recently opened a small finance consulting business in the city. I was proud of her; I even helped her pick out the office space.

"I have a few clients, but business is still growing since I just opened."

"Well, I'm sure you already have some great clients, other than myself."

"I really do. They make me excited to work. They're really good businesses. Since all three of them are women, and they have their own companies, it's nice to help them meet their financial goals."

It was nice to see Viv so excited about her company.

"What time is Damien going to get here?"

"He said he'll be here by six, so that I had time to cook. You're the one who wanted to get here extremely early." She laughed, and looked at her watch. It was a quarter to five.

"Well, Sin's mom came into town and kicked me out, so I had no place else to go." She came into the living room and handed me a bottle of water and a black folder.

"Her mom?" Viv's face was pure shock and amusement.

"Yes, her mom." I took my shoes off, and got comfortable on the sofa.

"What does she look like?"

"Really, Viv?" I couldn't stop myself from laughing; she had asked such a weird question.

"I seriously want to know." She placed her hands on her hips waiting for me to answer her question.

"She looks like an older woman." I didn't know how to describe Sin's mother.

"Is she pretty, Courtland?"

"Yes, I guess, she's a very nice looking woman." I wasn't sure how I was supposed to answer.

"Uh-huh?" She looked me up and down.

"Anyway, what's on the menu?"

"Lamb," she said excitedly. "For some strange reason, I've been craving lamb with butter and herbs. I found an amazing recipe on Pinterest, so I'm excited about trying it."

"Sounds like I should have eaten before I came." I was too hungry to have Viv playing with my food.

"Oh, be quiet." Viv left me downstairs and she headed upstairs. "I'm going to wash up so I can start dinner. Look over those numbers for your next project."

I opened up the folder and saw that she had drafted up numbers for the next three years, along with a five-year plan. I had put everything I had planned on hold, but I needed to get my business started.

"What you think?" Viv was skipping down the stairs in a colorful, flowing gown.

"What do you have on?" It looked like she was about to go to the beach.

"It's a lounge dress, but this ain't your concern." She twirled around in her outfit. "What do you think about those numbers?" She asked me again.

"How soon would I start getting my return on investment?"

"Within the first eight months, but that's only if you market correctly."

She went into the kitchen, and I could hear pans banging against one another. I was starting to feel nervous, because I wasn't sure if Viv knew what she was doing.

"Viv? You sure you don't want to order in?"

I jumped up when she walked back into the living room with a pan in her hand. She looked like she was ready to hit me on the head with it.

"You're gonna eat this damn lamb, and you gonna love it, understood?" She was standing over me with the pan in my face.

"You got it, Viv!"

I stood up and fixed my collar. I took a deep breath and she went back to the kitchen.

Viv went back to rummaging through the kitchen, and the doorbell rang. Clearly she wasn't going to get the door. I peeped out the front window, and saw Damien's car parked in the driveway behind mine's.

"Can you get that? It should be Damien."

I walked to the front door, and I could see Damien standing there.

"What's going on?" I opened the door, and we each other greeted with a hug.

"Nothing much at all." He stepped inside, and I closed the door behind him.

I pulled him back to me by his arm. "Have you eaten Viv's food before? I whispered to him.

"Yeah," he said trying to hold in his laughter.

"And it was good, right?" I needed reassurance. I was starving.

"Yeah, man." He patted my shoulder. "You have nothing to worry about."

We walked into the kitchen, and Damien began caressing Viv's neck.

"Umm, I think I'm going to leave." I had never seen any intimacy between them, and I wanted to keep it that way. Viv was my best friend; I didn't want any sexual pictures of her imprinted in my mind.

"Get out your feelings, Courtland." Viv rolled her eyes at me and laughed.

"Hey, man. I had something I wanted to talk to you about." Damien walked towards me and led me into the living room.

"What's up?"

"I can't find Victoria at all. She's completely off the grid." His eyes were wide as he whispered to me.

I had asked him to keep an eye on Victoria because I didn't trust her. She was given house arrest, but one night she disappeared, and everyone was looking for her.

"Well, let's just keep an eye out for her, just in case she does pop up. I don't trust her, and she's lost everything, and I know how vindictive she can be."

"Gotcha."

"Man." I took a deep breath, and leaned back on the sofa.

"Look, we not gonna stress this shit man." Damien was more like a brother to me these days. He really had my back these past few months, and he was my biggest supporter.

"You right, man." I knew he was. I couldn't focus on the negatives right now. I had a business to start, and I couldn't let anyone catch me slipping because I wasn't thinking clearly. I was already behind, and I didn't need any more unnecessary setbacks.

"So what's next? Have you gone by the Palace? It's looking good from what I could see last week when I rode by."

"Yeah, I have them adding a tennis court and a basketball court to the back. If I could buy more land, I would add a golf course, but that doesn't look like it can happen."

"Man, I can't wait!" He seemed genuinely excited about my newest venture.

Since I had put everything on hold with Sin, I had decided to turn the building into something like a country club, for city folks. There wasn't anything like it in Atlanta, so I knew it was a good move for business.

"Yeah, this is what your girl put together for me." I handed him the folder with my projected numbers.

He took his time reading over everything.

"All of this is legal, right?" He looked at me with the biggest grin on his face.

"Hell yeah! I refuse to get caught up in another scandal. I'm sure they're watching me like a hawk, trying to find something to use against me."

"Right," he agreed. "When do you open?"

"In exactly thirty days. Memberships are already being bought thanks to Jenna, so I know business will be booming."

"I know. I already know. Jenna is a really proactive part of this business, don't you think?"

"Hell yeah!" I couldn't hide my excitement. She had a great business mind, and she didn't mind calling shots, or telling me how things were going to work. I was really happy to know that she and Viv worked well together too.

Damien nodded his head in agreement.

"We need to hire bartenders, front desk personnel, and housekeepers." I was going to need his help with the fun part.

"We?" Damien laughed. "I didn't know you would be needing my services." He sat up straight with an attentive look on his face.

"Well, I thought you would enjoy this part of the process." I rubbed my hands together. "I know I am."

"I'm not a single man anymore, Courtland. You trying to make Viv poison me or something?" He whispered and we both laughed.

"I forgot you all are official now. Well, the offer is on the table, and I would rather have my right hand man assist me."

"Now you know I plan to be there every step of the way."

Viv walked into the living room with her beach gown on. "Dinner will be served after you all set the table."

"Dang, Viv, why you gotta be so extra?" I didn't want to set a table. Leave it to Viv to try and humble somebody.

"Everything is on the table, so when you all are done, I'll be ready to put the food out."

Everything was smelling good, and I didn't want to wait anymore. Damien and I got up and set the table like we were children.

"Damn you, Viviana!" I yelled so that she could hear me in the kitchen.

She laughed.

CHAPTER THREE

Sinaiyah

I woke up from my nap feeling good. I would have slept throughout the night had I not smelled something good cooking.

I walked into the kitchen, and my mother was bending over looking inside of the stove.

"Mom, what are you doing?" I meant to ask what was she cooking, but my mind was still gone.

"Cooking!" She turned around with a smile on her face. "You could use a good home-cooked meal."

"You brought your apron?" I didn't own any aprons, but my mother was standing in my kitchen with one on. I laughed on the inside, because she was acting like Mrs. Beaver.

"Of course, I did." She closed the oven, and wiped her hands with a napkin. "You woke up on time, too. The oxtails are almost done."

"Oxtails?" hearing that word made me instantly happy. I loved oxtails. That was the first thing I learned to cook in my grandmother's house because she loved them. I could picture them falling off the bones onto some white rice.

"You already know." She walked up towards me and pinched my check.

I walked to the cabinet above the refrigerator to my heavy liquor stash. I was going to grab a quick drink. I wasn't thirsty, and I didn't realize what I was doing. It had become second nature for me to grab a drink after I woke up.

"Mom! Where are my bottles?" My heart sunk into my stomach, and I immediately felt sick. None of my liquor was in the cabinet. I went to the side of the counter to see if I still had wine. My wine rack was still full. I was able to take a sigh of relief seeing all of my pretty bottles of wine.

"I hid them." She stopped stirring vegetables on the stove, and patted my hips, motioning for me to get up. She placed her hands on her hips. "You better be happy I didn't pour it out, and you better be happy I love wine, because as you see, I left you that."

I was heated, but I tried to catch myself. Alcohol was my newfound love, and I felt like my mother had invaded our privacy. I inhaled slowly and exhaled. I had to remind myself that I asked her to come, so I didn't need to be rude to her.

"So how long are you going to be here?" I knew she was only trying to help me, but I could see I wasn't going to want her in my space for too long.

"Well, you know I'm going to be here at least until you open your wellness center, and get comfortable in your business. Is that fine with you?"

Sarcasm was all over her tone, and her head was tilted to the side.

"Yeah. Oh, okay then." I smiled and nodded my head. I walked back over to the refrigerator to close the cabinet doors that I had left open.

She grabbed a glass from the dishwasher, poured me a glass of water, and handed it to me. "When was the last time you had some of this in your body?"

I took the glass and drank the water. It felt weird on my tongue. I remember when all I would drink was water with an occasional glass of lemonade, but now it had been a long time since I had last drank water. I wasn't satisfied with the water and I'm sure it showed on my face.

"Yeah, take a seat, and I'll bring you a plate." She took the oxtails out of the oven and turned it off.

"Thanks, Mom, I appreciate it." I didn't want her to feel like I didn't want her here, because I did.

I took a seat at the head of my dining room table. I hadn't used this table for eating yet, but had planned on hosting dinners one day. The last time I used it, Courtland had me bent over it in my favorite position.

"You know I want to be here." Her back was facing me, as she finished getting everything together.

"Well, I'm happy you're here." I felt like I couldn't say it enough. I had never had a real relationship with my mom, so I was happy that she wanted to be here and take care of me.

"Oh, before I forget, I put your phone in your bedroom. It kept ringing, and I didn't know how to put it on silent." She brought me a big plate of food, placed a wine glass to my right, and one where she would be sitting.

"Oh." I was responding so that she knew that I heard her. I didn't care. I wasn't in the mood to talk to anyone anyway, and it probably was Courtland.

"Someone named Viviana called, and then Landon kept calling. He's the reason why I put your phone in the back." She came into the dining area, placed her plate on the table, and went back to the kitchen.

I rolled my eyes, because I already knew where this conversation was headed. My mother loved Landon. When we were younger, I tried to keep our relationship private, but she and his mom were best friends, so of course, she found out about Landon and I dating. I was thankful that she didn't tell my grandmother, because I wasn't allowed to date in her house.

"Well, thank you for thinking of me." I wanted to change the subject, but I didn't have anything else to talk about.

"Well," She came back, and paused as she poured us both a glass of wine. "Have you spoken to him?"

"Nope."

"You sound like you don't plan on talking to him." A look of disappointment crossed her face, as she took her seat beside me.

"I'm still trying to figure everything out."

"Like what? I remember when you were head over heels in love with him."

"Yeah, well life keeps going, whether you love someone or not." I didn't think she needed to be reminded of that, but maybe she did. I hated she wasn't taking the hint that I didn't want to talk about him.

"You sound upset. Did anything else happen?" She was prying too much.

"I would rather not talk about it."

Honestly, it wasn't any of her business what I decided to do with Landon. He had hurt me in the past, but it didn't compare to the hurt he caused to Courtland by befriending to get to me. I didn't know that I meant anything to him. I had written him letters, and tried calling him multiple times when I was in college, but he never picked up or wrote back. I didn't understand why my mother was so interested in our relationship, but she needed to get over it. I was already over him. I didn't need his energy in my life. I was trying to keep my aura positive, so that I could receive the blessings that I knew were on the way for me. I wasn't the most spiritual person, but I had been through enough shit to know that after every storm comes the sun and a rainbow, and my business was going to be my rainbow, and its success was going to be my sun.

"Calm down, because we are going to talk about this. You need to cleanse your heart so that you can make way for bigger and better blessings in your life. No need for you to be holding on to resentment. It won't do you no good. Trust me."

"I'm not holding on to any resentment." I took my time eating my food, because I could feel myself getting full. I wasn't mad. I just knew what I wasn't going to allow, and that was Landon and whatever he had planned for us.

"Okay, so let's talk. How did you feel when you saw him?"

"My heart skipped a beat." There was no point in lying. I was surprised to see him. I hadn't prepared myself for the possibility of ever seeing him again.

"Uh-huh, and…"

"Honestly, I didn't think I would see him again. I won't say I forgot about him, but I pushed him to the back of my thoughts."

"Okay, so that's how you coped with his absence, nothing wrong with that."

"Mommy, I never heard from him." I was trying not to cry, because I was still hurt by his rejection. "I called and called. I even wrote him a letter, and I never heard from him. Then he comes back into my life, like he's Mr. Everything, and he is. He's doing well for himself. I loved him, but he abandoned me, and that's unforgivable."

I was crying, he broke my heart, and I never dealt with it. He was out of sight, out of mind. I wrote it off because it was a high school fling. Nothing serious. I wasn't sure what I was expecting from him. We were both young and had a lot of growing up to do. I remember feeling like he didn't care about me, like maybe I was just something to do to pass time. We did live in the country, where nothing much ever happened.

"Okay, so now he's back. What are you going to do? No need in abandoning him. Give him what you deserved: honesty."

"It's fine. Plus, I've moved on anyway, so it doesn't matter."

"Oh, honey, your heart hasn't moved anywhere, but back in time. If you were over him, this conversation would have gone completely different and you wouldn't be crying." She wiped my face with her index finger.

I wasn't expecting her to have an adult conversation with me. All my life I wanted a relationship with her, and it was finally happening. I couldn't help but smile. Despite the topic of conversation, I was in a happy place.

"I'll figure it out." I picked my fork back up and finished eating.

"But it's okay if you don't." Concern was in her eyes. "You just have to make sure that you're okay. You have to protect you, because no one else can."

"You're right." That was the lesson I had learned through everything with Courtland and his mother's company. I cried a few more silent tears, because it felt like God was giving me confirmation about where I was in this moment. I was exactly where I needed to be.

"Okay, so talk to me about Dr. Beauty. I plan to help you run this business."

"Oh, I want you to! We have to put that business degree to use." I winked at her.

"Exactly!" she winked back at me.

CHAPTER FOUR

Courtland

"Hello, my name is Jenna Crawford, and I will be overseeing your interviews. There are a lot of you, and we will not need all of you, so I'm sure I don't have to tell you to bring your A-game. You'll have two minutes to prepare two drinks of your choice for the two gentlemen behind me. You need to communicate with a server in getting your drinks to their table, and to the right person in an orderly fashion. Your servers are Maya and Angie. Okay! First up are Josie, Anna, and Melanie. Let's begin." She walked to the end of the bar, and took her seat. "You can start."

"She is killing it." Damien leaned over to me. I was happy that he made it. I wasn't sure if he was going to help pick out the rest of the staff. He had put a nice sum of money to invest in this business with me, and I wanted him to feel he was a valued part of this company.

"Yeah, and can you believe she's never done anything like this before?" I laughed.

"Wow." He leaned back in his chair in amazement. "She's good."

The inside of the Courtland Palace was just about complete, and we were making great progress. I had hired Jenna last month to be my personal assistant, and she jumped right in, without me having to give her any real direction. I met her at an event and through small talk I found out that she had recently graduated with a degree in marketing and was looking for a job. She asked if I needed a personal assistant, and at that time I felt like I didn't. After talking it over with Viv, she encouraged me to hire her, and I'm glad I did. Jenna took a lot of stress off of me. Within two weeks of her starting, we already had a maid staff, four massage therapists, servers, and hostesses. I decided to hire Dawn as my front desk manager, and she worked well with Jenna.

"Time's up," Jenna said, signaling the young ladies to stop.

"Thanks, Angie." She brought us the first round of drinks, and the presentation was impeccable. I couldn't wait to sample their drinks.

My taste buds shot through the roof when I tasted my drink. I looked over at Damien and he was just as happy as I was. We pounded fists in agreement. We both could get used to this. The first group did an excellent job on their drinks. I was excited, because more were to come.

Damien and I were feeling good by the end of the interviews. We decided on seven girls to start with: Melanie, Simone, Valerie, Nicole, Sherae, Katy, and

Jordyn. Jenna chose an older lady named Natalia to be the manager. They filled out all of the necessary forms and left with their training dates. Things moved so quickly with Jenna because she was organized.

"Good job today, Jenna." She took a seat at the table with us, looking exhausted.

"You happy with the girls?" She leaned her arms on the table. The sparkle in her dark brown eyes was gone, so I knew it was time for her to clock out.

"Yup. We'll probably need to hire a few more, but I think this is a great start." I gave her a high five. She was working hard, and I appreciated her. She had proven that she could handle any task given to her.

"That's all that matters." She smiled, and put her head down on the table.

"Well, you go home and get some rest. You can have tomorrow off. You've been working your ass off." Jenna hadn't taken a day off since she started, and I didn't need her to burn out before we officially opened.

She raised her head, looking at me and Damien. "Well, don't y'all stay out too late." She stood up and headed to the storage closet behind the bar to grab her stuff before she left.

We heard the door slam. It was nice to sit in the empty Palace and see how far we had gotten in such a small amount of time.

"I'm still in awe of her." Damien was pleased with her efficiency the entire time. I had told him about Jenna and some of the work she had done, but today was his first time seeing her in action.

"Me too, she's doing a soft open in about another week or so, which is why she's been working so hard. She's been working with my webmaster, and they've developed some really amazing marketing strategies. I'm just happy that memberships have been selling consistently."

"And she's only been working for a week?" He seemed shocked.

"She dove in head first. That's why I told her to go home and rest, she hasn't taken a day off yet."

"Oh, she's the real deal." He nodded his head in approval.

"Yeah! Once they finished the outside, she had a photo-shoot. I don't know who took the photos, but they are amazing. I can see why people are jumping on the memberships." I was so excited I couldn't stop talking. What I appreciated about Jenna was that she had vision, and I didn't realize how important of a quality that was to have. She knew what I wanted and she was able to develop and produce the best results.

"How many members do you have?" He was still drinking his last drink.

"Just a little over two hundred. She's marketing this as an exclusive city club for the upper elite, for both men and women, and it's working. She's bringing us all of the right attention."

"Really?"

"Yeah, she's giving nice incentives to our members, which is really why they are signing up. We're even gearing up for a New Year's eve party that I'm excited about."

"I'm happy to have her on our team then. I want to hear more about this party. No! I need to hear more, because I plan to shut it down." Damien raised his glass to mine.

"You and me both." We finished our drinks laughing.

"Have you spoken to Sin?"

I hesitated. I hadn't talked about her much. I was trying to keep myself busy in my newest venture. She needed time away from me, and I was giving her all of the space she needed.

"No, I haven't. Have you?" I was being facetious.

"Of course not, but you know she's Viv client, so she comes around every so often. She has her grand-opening coming up in another week. Are you going?"

"Wait, when did Sin become a client of Viv's?" I was confused. I didn't know how could Sin trust Viv, especially since they hadn't known each other for long. Viv hadn't even told me that Sin was a client of hers.

"I'm not sure, but she is, and Jaslynn is working with Sin now. That's who Jenna reminds me of. She's just a little younger. They're both pretty young." Damien was continuing with his conversation, but I was still stuck on Viv and her clients.

I couldn't believe what he was telling me. I was trying to keep a straight face, but I was upset. Viv didn't tell me that she had taken on my ex-girlfriend as her client. I couldn't be mad at Viv; Sin was good for business. I mean, I helped her business, but I didn't like the secrecy.

"But are you going to stop by her grand opening?" Damien asked me again. I had stopped listening to him, because I was consumed with my own thoughts.

"Yeah, I plan to stop by." I began rambling. "Sin's my heart, I definitely will be there to support her." I shifted in my chair. "Alright, let's get out of here, I have an errand I need to run."

"Cool." Damien got up from his seat, and I took our glasses over to the sink behind the bar.

I turned off the lights and we headed out of the Palace. "Talk to you later, bro." I hopped in my truck, and he got in his car and pulled off.

I didn't have any errands to run, I just needed a moment alone. Viv and Sin were closer than I thought, and my relationship with Sin seemed to be coming to an end. I rolled down my window and headed to the bar down the street. I didn't need anything else to drink, but I didn't want to go home just yet.

The bar was packed with women, it had to be ladies' night or something, but I didn't mind. There was a DJ booth set up across from the bar, and he had a long line of ladies waiting. I headed straight to the bar and ordered a drink. I took a seat and stared at one of the televisions. It was football season, so there were two different games showing on both televisions.

"Y'all give it up for Stephanie." He laughed into the microphone.

I turned around to see what was going on. It was karaoke night, which explained the long line of women at the booth. Stephanie was a cute, brown haired girl with freckles and big curly hair. She looked exotic, but sexy nonetheless, and she was completely drunk.

"I'm getting tired of yo shit!" She started singing. I had never been to a bar that did karaoke. Stephanie was funny standing up there giving the performance of her life. She couldn't sing worth a lick, but she was engaging. I couldn't take my eyes off of her. She looked at me and pointed. "You betta call Tyrone." I looked from side to side. I didn't want her drawing any more attention to me, so I nodded my head, took a sip of my drink, and asked the bar tender for another round.

"You must be new around town." A beautiful Asian woman sat down beside me.

"No, but I am new here." I turned towards her. She moved in between my legs and placed her hand on my thigh.

My name is Sakaë. Yours?" She had a devilish grin on her face, but it was sexy.

"Courtland." I held my hand out so that we could formally greet each other. Instead she grabbed my hand, and placed it on her waist. Her figure was petite, compared to what I was used to, but her legs were long, and that was a weakness of mine.

"What an uncommon name." She rested both of her hands on my thighs.

"Your name is very exotic." I leaned back in my chair and she brought herself closer to me.

"It means prosperity."

"Well, I like to prosper." I took a sip of my drink.

"As do I." She snickered to herself. "So tell me about yourself, Courtland." She looked at me with lustful eyes. She didn't give a damn about me. She wanted to fuck, and I was ready.

"Okay. I'm a businessman, born and raised in Atlanta. Your turn." She began stroking my dick through my pants. I touched her arm, because my dick was hard, and I was ready for her to feel it.

"I'm your dream come true." She turned around and motioned towards the area where the restrooms were. "Meet me back there in five minutes."

I nodded and she walked off. I wasn't sure what I was about to get myself into, and it didn't matter. I was going to finish my drink and walk my ass to the back and meet her. I reached in my back pocket, and pulled out my wallet. I had placed two new condoms in it just in case. I put one in my front pocket for easy access.

I finished my second round of drinks and paid. I got up from the bar to start making my way to the back. People were standing up dancing and drinking, having a great ole time as I slipped off to the back.

"I thought you had changed your mind for a second." Sakaë was standing against the back wall. Her body was shapelier than I had given her credit.

"Nah, I was obeying your orders. You said five minutes right?" I looked down at my watch. I was right on time.

"So you're good at taking orders, huh?" She had a smirk on her face.

"If I benefit from them." I walked towards her and she went down the hall. I followed her. She quietly opened a back room door and stepped inside after turning on the light. I walked in behind her and she locked the door behind me. It was an office but it looked like nobody did any real business in here.

"Well, here's another order: have your way with me." She pulled the bow from her dress and it unwrapped instantly.

I picked her up by her butt and kissed her hard. "Certainly."

She placed her arms around my neck and she pulled me closer to her with her legs. I pinned her up against the wall and pulled out the condom. I hurriedly placed it on my hard dick and slid her down my shaft. Her walls were so tight, I gasped.

"Damn." She moaned out. I could tell she was trying to hold back from screaming as I shoved myself in and out of her. She grabbed the handle on the wall to catch herself. I kissed her nipples lightly at first, and then I bit and sucked them hard. I could feel her hand on the back of my neck. She arched her back as she came all over my dick.

"Mmmhmm." I put her back down, and turned her around and bent her over. It felt good to be in some new pussy. I hit her with a long stroke and she tightened her walls and I loved that shit. I bent over her, trying to catch myself from nutting, now was not the time. I rose back up and watched her as she bounced back and forth on my dick. I was about to nut and she could tell. She pulled herself off of me, and grabbed the condom. She swallowed my hard dick whole and I couldn't believe it. I leaned back on the wall, and busted all over her mouth and chin.

I zipped my pants up, and bent down and picked her dress from the floor.

"How do you feel?"

"Like my dream just came true." I told her. I didn't have much else to say, while I was in orgasmic bliss.

CHAPTER FIVE

Sinaiyah

I couldn't stop fidgeting. I was straight up nervous.

I hadn't seen Landon since our little "reunion," and here he was sitting right in front of me, and I can't even look at him.

I still couldn't believe that this time had come. In college, I would imagine what I would say to him whenever I saw him. I never knew if I would curse him out, or kiss him so deeply, we would go back in time.

"You look beautiful, my lady." Landon broke my thoughts. He was trying to get me to look at him, but I couldn't. Deep down, I still cared about him; I probably still loved him, I just didn't want to admit it to myself.

"Thank you, Landon." I took a sip of my water, trying to calm my nerves. Too bad I had stopped drinking…for the most part. My mother was weaning me slowly off the heavy liquor, even though I didn't appreciate it. I looked outside the window; it was a beautiful day today. I guess we had broken the ice, but I still felt awkward in front of him. I really couldn't believe I was sitting in front of him, willingly.

"So I hear you're the new doctor of beauty." I could see him smiling at me out the corner of my eye.

"Yeah, I'm something like that." I giggled. I didn't want to bring any man of mine into my company's business, but it was nice that he had done a little research on my next move. I guess word was getting out, thanks to Jaslynn. It was nice of him to keep up with what I was doing.

"No need to be shy." He touched the back of my hand, and his touch immediately sent shivers down my spine. "I know it's been a while since we last saw each other, and even longer since we spent time together, but I still love you all the same."

I wasn't sure how I was supposed to take his statement. I'm sure that was easy for him to say. He spoke as if I did him wrong, and he had forgiven me, when in actuality he had done me wrong, and I had not completely forgiven him. I didn't trust him. I was still disappointed in him, and how he handled our situation.

"You love me all the same, huh?" I looked at him with a slight frown on my face. I wanted to make him uncomfortable, and by the way he shifted in his seat, I knew I had succeeded.

"Yes, Sinaiyah, I do." He was clearly trying to force this answer out of his mouth.

"That's nice to know, but I still am unsure about this." I felt the need to be honest with him, since he was attempting to be honest with me.

Truth be told, my mother had to force me to go out with him, because he wouldn't stop calling. I didn't want to see him; I was hoping he would get the hint and leave me alone, but he became more persistent. I was nervous about him, because something didn't seem right, and one thing I had learned from dealing with Courtland was to trust my own feelings.

"I can understand why you're hesitating." He leaned back in his seat to get comfortable. "You're worth waiting for, so I have no problem proving myself and my love for you." His stare was serious.

I wanted to tell him that all of that wasn't necessary. I had made the decision to stay focused on me at the moment. This for me was a courtesy dinner, especially since he was making it a point for me to see him. I couldn't blame him, since we had unfinished business, and one thing my grandmother always used to say was that *'unfinished business always has a way of finishing itself,'* and boy, was she right. My unfinished business had found me, and was now sitting smack dead in front of me, and I wasn't ready.

"So what's new with you? You seem to be doing well for yourself these days."

"I'm just a regular attorney, trying to make a name for myself," he said, blushing.

"Oh, really? So it took you this long to find me because you were trying to be just a 'regular attorney.'" I looked at him, waiting for an answer to the low blow I had just given him.

He looked down and smiled. He had known it was coming. I didn't give a damn about who he was to the outside world, or what he was doing these days. I cared about what took him so long to come for me, and why he felt he had to manipulate people to get to me.

I would never forget how we made plans to run off together. We were so young and in love, and I knew we would be okay. We had just graduated from high school and I had already been accepted into the State's University, and at the time, he had plans of joining the military. The night we planned to run away, he was a no show, and had left me a letter under a stairway we used to meet late at night to make-out. I still had the letter saved in my journal, because I always believed he would be back. So when he didn't come for me, I had to accept it and move on. I cried so many nights, because he was gone.

"I can't explain why it took me so long to come to you."

"Because you didn't really want me, that's the real answer." I cut him off before he could say anymore. I didn't care to hear any of his lies. "I waited and waited for you. I called and I even wrote you letters." I was trying to stay calm. I needed to make sure I was thinking clearly at all times with him.

"I got your letters." His voice was stern and matter-of-fact.

"And you never responded," I shouted. My blood was boiling. Everyone in the café looked towards us, but

I didn't care; I was furious. "I knew this was a bad idea. I can't do this with you." I pushed my chair back, and stood up. "Please do not contact me again. I don't know what you're trying to prove to yourself, because you damn sure ain't trying to prove nothing to me, but we can never be anything more than childhood friends."

I grabbed my purse from the chair next to me, placed it on my right shoulder, and headed for the door. I was hurt. He was my first love, and he was playing with my emotions. I wasn't who he wanted. If he really wanted me, he would have called me back and responded to my letters. If he really wanted me, he would have never allowed me to feel like he didn't want me.

"Hey, Ma, are you dressed?" I called her as soon as I walked out of the café. I stood waiting for the valet to bring my car around.

"Why are you calling me? You should still be at lunch." She ignored my question.

"Ma! Are you dressed?" I didn't mean yell at her, but I was still agitated by Landon and his nonchalant responses.

"What happened at lunch? You walked out on him, didn't you? I knew you would."

"Lunch didn't go as planned." I answered her, because she had no intention of answering my question. I hoped in my car, and sped off. "I'm leaving the café now, and I'm heading home to get you so that we can meet Jaslynn at the office."

"I'm ready. I'll be downstairs when you pull up." She sounded defeated.

"Awesome. I'll be there in ten minutes."

"Yes ma'am." I could tell she was biting her tongue on this issue.

"And, Mom, I don't want to talk about what happened at lunch when I get you."

"That's fine." I could tell she had an attitude.

I hung up the phone and headed to the house to pick her up so that we could head to my new office to check on Jaslynn and the big furniture shipment that I was expecting at any moment.

When I pulled up to the front of my building, my mom was waiting outside for me. She was cute with her shades on and her big curly fro.

"How are you, young lady?" She closed the door behind her and put her seat belt on.

"Good, and you?" I asked to be polite.

"I'm fantastic."

"That's good to hear."

"So what's new with you?"

"Oh, nothing. Anything new with you?"

"Nope."

My mom was being a smart ass about the situation, but I refused to talk about Landon.

We pulled up to my office and the deliverymen were unloading the truck.

"That goes into the conference room, all the way in the back." Jaslynn was telling the movers that were carrying black chairs.

"Hey, my dear, how's moving going?"

Jaslynn was dressed in leggings and a crop top. She was ready for today, with her tennis shoes and bottle of water.

"Girl, you are working me to death." We both laughed. I enjoyed Jaslynn so much. She had really become a rock in my life. "But, no, they finished painting yesterday. I think you're going to love the color scheme. I know you said you wanted dainty-professional, and I think I achieved that for you."

I let Jaslynn have her way with the front area, since that was going to be her area. She had really good taste. Together we had gone over color schemes for the other offices, and conference room. My only rule was no white walls.

"Oh, my goodness, this is going to be gorgeous." My mom's mouth was wide open. She was enamored by the rose-colored walls, high ceilings, and the shelves behind the desk. The front desk was white, with a beautiful pewter chair behind it, and a vase with flowers were sitting pretty, ready to bloom.

"I love what you did to your little area." I teased Jaslynn. Momma was right. It was gorgeous. I couldn't wait to see the finished product.

"Me too." She giggled. I was happy that I could make her happy. I was cutting her a nice little check, but she was making my money worthwhile.

She gave me a tour as best as she could with the men moving items into the designated spaces. I was really happy that my little project was coming to life. We sat down to discuss the plan for the upcoming brunch. I was more than ready to get this show started.

CHAPTER SIX

Courtland

Sin and I had been texting for the past couple of hours. She wanted to see me and get a tour of the Palace. I wasn't trying to keep it from her, but I didn't want her to know much about my new venture. It had turned into a bittersweet moment. I had built this place for us, and now she had nothing to do with it. I didn't want her to be a stranger in my building; I wanted her to feel like it was hers—like it was ours.

"You need a drink, boss?" I looked up and saw Simone wiping down the counter behind the bar.

"No, don't worry yourself" I looked down at my watch; it was almost midnight. "Did you give the last drop to Jenna?"

"Yes, sir." She rinsed out the towel that she used to wipe the counter down with.

"You can go ahead and leave. I'll finish up." I leaned back in my seat at the bar.

"You sure, Mr. Biggs? I'm sorry if I offended you."

"No, Simone," I laughed. She looked so worried. "You did absolutely nothing wrong. I'm just expecting a special guest tonight. It's not a big issue. You can stay if you like, but you don't have to. Is that better?" I wanted to ease her mind. I'd hate for her to think she was about to get fired for something crazy. She was actually a great worker and I enjoyed having her on our staff.

"Oh, okay, sir. I'll give you your space. I'll be out in the next minute." She walked over to the sink, quickly washed her hands, opened up the storage room, grabbed her purse, and left.

I took a deep breath and went behind the bar to pour myself a glass of whiskey. I didn't need it; I wanted it. My nerves were slightly off knowing that Sin was on her way. We were doing well at keeping our distance. I was surprised to receive a message from her the other day. I was even more surprised when she said that she wanted to see me. I really missed my woman.

"Hey!" Jenna came around the corner, and stood across from me at the bar.

"Hey, ma'am." I took a sip from my glass.

"I'm about to head out, I'll be in early tomorrow, and I'll go to the bank in the morning."

"Sounds good to me."

"Everything okay?" she asked.

"Yeah, I'm fine. Can you email me an updated list of accounts?"

"I sure can, and if you need anything, don't hesitate to ask." She touched the back of my hand.

I nodded my head. "Good, and I'm fine. For real." I reassured her.

"Whatever you say." She threw her hands up before she left for the evening.

I turned on the alarm system from my phone, and sent the call button to my phone. That way I would know when Sin pulled up to the gate.

I walked around the bar and took a seat. I had to get my thoughts together before Sin got here.

I wondered how her business was going. Sin was a phenomenal woman in my eyes. I hate that we had been through so many ups and downs, but I never thought that we wouldn't get through it. I always thought Sin would be mine. I wasn't used to her feeling like a stranger, and I never wanted that for us. I wanted us to be together so badly. I loved her so much.

I sat at the bar and thought about what would have happened if I had shown her that I loved her when we were together. I tried my best to take my time with her, and show her my appreciation of her, but I wasn't sure if I had succeeded in my efforts.

My phone vibrated to let me know that someone was at the gate. I immediately press the code so that Sin could come through.

I hurried and swallowed the rest of my whiskey and rinsed the glass out. I took a deep breath and shook all of the nervous tension from my body. I walked to the main area near the front door. I didn't know if I should try and look busy, or if I should wait by the door. I hadn't seen Sin since I left her house a few weeks ago when her mom first arrived. I had given her some space, and I had been waiting patiently for her to reach out to me.

I was caught off guard when I heard a knock at the door.

I rushed to the door and opened it.

Sin was standing at the door looking drop dead gorgeous. Her hair was down and she was glowing. She was wearing a tan colored lace dress, and it fit in all of my favorite places.

"So are you going to invite me in?" she asked politely.

I had to catch my breath. I stepped to the side, so that she could walk in.

"You know you're the only one who has ever knocked on this door for entry." I watched her hips sway from side to side. Her walk was rhythmic, and sensual. Every time she walked into a room, I could just stare. I closed the door behind her, and walked up next to her.

"Well, I don't know how things work around here. I don't want to mess up your flow." She turned towards me and smiled.

"You couldn't do that, when you're a part of my flow."

She blushed. I was enjoying this moment. It had been so long since I saw the woman I had once fallen in love with. It was nice to see her back to herself and not falling over intoxicated.

"Would you like anything to drink?" I hated to ask her. I missed this Sin that was standing in front of me. Plus, I would rather have all of her attention.

"Water, please." She smiled.

"I'm really glad you said that." We both laughed. I placed my hand on her lower back and pulled her towards me. I hugged her as tight as I possibly could without making it hard for her to breath.

We were the only ones in the building, and I was happy to have my woman to myself. A lot had happened to us and I appreciated this moment.

I let her go and looked at her dark brown eyes. I had missed her for so long. I waited for this moment of sobriety for so long, and I refused to give up on her. I knew she was going to get through the hurt of everything.

I grabbed two glasses from the back, and filled them both with ice water.

"So how have you been?" I gave her a glass.

She took a sip and took her time answering the question.

"I've been really good." She nodded her head. "How have you been?"

"Awesome, babe, I've been awesome. You stopped drinking?"

"For the most part, I have, but don't think I'm giving up my wine." She raised her glass to mine and laughed. She seemed so innocent. I wanted to protect her, and I only wanted her for myself. I didn't want to share her with this mean world again; it had damaged her.

"Well, you look great too," I had to give her credit where it was due.

"Thank you, baby." She touched her dress.

"Can your baby get a kiss?" I couldn't resist asking. I felt like I had to. I felt like I would be disrespecting her if I just expected one.

"I don't know about that," she said, laughing.

I gave her a sad look to show my hurt. I couldn't remember the last time I kissed her.

"Well, just know I'll be waiting for one." I took a big gulp of water. I wasn't ready for the rejection.

"I will dance with you." She smiled.

I was confused by her offer, there wasn't any music playing, but knowing her she probably had a tune in her head.

"Okay." I accepted her offer before she could take it back. At this point, I would do anything to hold her in my arms.

I stood up, and held up a finger to her. I ran to the storage room and turned the iPod player on. I settled for some smooth jazz, because I didn't have time to waste to pick a song.

I closed the door behind me and dimmed the lights. I approached Sin like a true gentleman. I wanted her to feel as comfortable as possible. She uncrossed her legs and stepped down from the bar chair. She couldn't stop smiling, and I was happy to know I was the reason for such a pretty smile.

I embraced Sin closely, and she wrapped both arms around my neck. It felt like it had been an eternity since she had held me. We didn't speak any words. We just stayed in sync with each other as the music played through the loud speakers.

"I love you, Sin." I whispered in her ear.

"I love you too, Courtland." She placed her head on my chest.

I didn't want our slow dance to come to an end, but I knew the song was almost over, and although the next song would play immediately, it didn't mean that Sin would be interested in another dance.

As the song was ending, Sin pulled away from me. I felt like I was in a losing battle. I let go of her waist and tried to force a smile.

"Thank you for the dance. It meant everything to me." She stared into my eyes.

I didn't want to look at her anymore. I wasn't sure what to do next. I didn't expect us to slow dance in the middle of the café.

"Of course," I wanted to choose my words carefully. "It meant even more to me."

I looked at the side of her face. I couldn't get lost in her big brown eyes again.

Sin grazed my cheek with the back of her hand; she was so warm. She turned my face towards hers, so that I could look her in her eyes.

"We're going to be okay." She placed my face in between both of her palms. "Trust me."

I leaned down towards her and kissed her gently on the lips. It was all I needed.

She took a step back from me and giggled. "You're so slick." she kept giggling.

"Well…"

"Moving on, are you going to give me a tour, or what?" She was so enthusiastic.

"Sure, anything for you." I reached out for her hand, and she placed her left hand in mine and followed my lead. It was good to have my woman back.

CHAPTER SEVEN

Sinaiyah

The Courtland Palace was absolutely stunning. When I pulled into the parking lot, I was ready to move in and claim my throne. It was so glamorous it looked like it was straight out of a magazine.

I wanted to know more about the building and why he chose to open this type of business. I wanted to know everything, but I kept many of my questions to myself, as I didn't want to come across too nosey.

"So if you ever want to take a break from your crazy schedule, you can come here to relax." We were leaving the poolroom. It was just as nice, with its own private bar area.

"I see." I looked around to peek in another room that was in the hallway.

"That's where we cater different parties. If you want to have an invite only party, we can make that happen." He was laying out the red carpet for me on this tour, and I was enjoying hearing him speak.

"Really?" That sounded like something that I would be interested in.

"Yes, ma'am." He had the widest smile on his face.

"This is really cool. I love this for you." I looked at him and nodded my head in approval, not that he needed it.

"Thank you, ma'am." He took a bow in the middle of the hallway.

It had been a long time since I had been around Courtland and I was happy I could enjoy him while I was sober. I could still feel the way his arms were wrapped around my waist when we slow danced. I was already missing being in his arms. I had no problem with following his lead this time around for a tour. Honestly, I missed following his lead, or at least being stubborn about following his lead. I didn't want to let his hand go, as we continued walking around the building. He smelled so good, and seeing him so confident made me want him even more. That was one of his strong qualities I was attracted to. I could tell he was really proud of himself, and I was proud, too.

"So what's downstairs?" I asked as we approached the stairwell in the back of the building. We had toured the entire main floor, and we even stepped outside for him to show me some of the outside amenities he offered his guests. He didn't want to go upstairs and I didn't pressure him about it. He told me it was unfinished, and that right now they were using the space for offices.

"I'll have more fun showing you." He squeezed my hand, and I smiled even harder. My cheeks were starting to hurt because I couldn't stop smiling.

"Sure you will." I was excited to find out what else was in this building.

He took the lead heading downstairs, and I wanted him bad. I was trying to be a good girl, and take things slow but I was ready to jump on top of him and at least ride his face for old time's sake. That's the least he deserved.

We took our time heading downstairs. "So how is everything coming together with you?" He glanced back at me.

"Everything is good. Getting ready for my opening, which is really exciting." I was happy about what I was doing, but compared to the Palace, I wasn't doing much of anything.

"I'm really proud of you, you know?" He stopped at the end of the stairs and turned around to me.

I could see that he was being genuine. His eyes were still as clear as the ocean blue. "Awe, that means so much to me. I'm really proud of you, too."

I met him at the bottom of the stairs and all I could do was gasp. It was just as beautiful as the upstairs. It was dimmer down here, but this was the relaxing area of the Palace. I walked up to the center table and touched the centerpiece of fresh flowers. I walked around the table one good time, and looked back at Courtland. The Palace was huge. I knew he had taken his time with this project. Now, I was wondering how long he had been working on this. I wasn't sure how he was able to afford this, because it looked like millions of dollars had been invested in this building and the many amenities that it offered.

"Welcome to my spa." He held his hands up.

There were different saunas to choose from, and two massage therapy rooms that had four beds each, one for women the other for men, and a separate locker-room area. There was another room strictly for feet and hand massages, and I couldn't wait to try the steam room. I was ready to get naked now and try out the different saunas at least.

"Tell me what you think." Courtland grabbed my hand and stood in front of me.

"I think it's amazing." I couldn't hide my feelings about his accomplishment. "Are the saunas working?" I didn't mean to be so forward, but I was ready.

"Yes, they work, but we haven't turned them on just yet. We're turning them on next week. You want to see the insides of them?"

"Yes," I squealed.

We walked into the first sauna room that was the closest to the entryway. I wasn't sure what this sauna was specifically for, but it was a small, quaint space, perfect for relaxing. Courtland pulled out two mats for us to sit on. I took my heels off, and sat in front of him.

"So do I get another kiss for good luck?" He asked with a confused look on his face.

"Come here." I threw my arms up and gave him a kiss. I was trying to stay strong, but I hadn't had any sexual release in a long time, and I was aching for him.

"I feel like I'm winning right now." He smiled at me.

"You are." I couldn't help myself, so I gave him another kiss.

He could tell I was hot and ready. He slipped me out of my dress really quickly and began caressing my body. I didn't realize how much I really missed his touch until I could feel his bare hands on my skin.

He pulled me to his lap and held me in his arms for a moment in silence. I think he needed a moment just like me. We had been through so much this past year. Everything had happened so fast, I didn't even really know where we stood. We never officially broke up. I went on a downward spiral, and I think we just assumed it was best for us to leave each other alone. That's when I had decided to cleanse myself of him, which didn't really go as planned.

I came to see him tonight, to be in his arms one more time. I needed to feel safe again. I had been hiding behind the liquor for so long that I felt vulnerable without it, and I needed my knight. I had told him we would be okay, because we always worked it out. I wasn't sure what was going to happen next, but I was ready for us to figure out our next step. I felt silly for wanting us to get back together. Courtland wasn't really acting like he wanted to fix us. He was moving on to his own ventures and I couldn't be any more proud of him.

He lifted my face to his and began kissing me. He took off his shirt and tie, and opened my legs. My body tingled as he kissed my inner thighs and I laid back on the mat. I felt like I was about to explode. I started trying to push his head to my clit, but he wasn't having that. He wanted me to squirm, and that's what I did. I left myself up to his face trying to feel his tongue on the inside of me, but he kept teasing me.

He finally placed his tongue inside of me, and I could feel my wetness flow from me. I could feel him making circles around my clit. He bit my clit softly, and sucked the life out of me. I arched my back so that he could taste every drop. I didn't want him to stop. The tingling sensation didn't stop. I could feel it from the inside out.

He got up and his mouth was soaking wet just the way I liked it. He took his pants off, and began slowly stroking me until he was deep inside of me. He kissed me hard, and I was able to lick my juices from his face. I held him by the lower part of his back. He felt so good inside of me; he was the perfect fit. He came quickly, which was fine with me.

I grabbed his penis and began stroking it while I licked his balls. I could hear him trying to hold back his moans. I swallowed his dick with my mouth, and he placed his hand on the back of my head. He was cursing under his breath and I sucked harder, forcing his dick up and down my throat. I could feel myself ready to gag, but I didn't stop sucking. I wanted him to feel how much I missed him. His veins started pulsating inside my mouth, which meant he came. I slurped him up and he spun me around while I was on my hands and knees. I was ready for nut number three; it was my favorite.

I stuck my finger inside my vagina because I was so wet. "Move." He smacked my hand out of the way. I didn't have anything to say. He wasted no more time. He positioned himself inside of me, and held me by my hips. He gave me long, strong strokes. His dick was so wet; it was overflowing with my juices. He pulled out of me, and sucked my clit again, and I came all over his face. I couldn't move. He smacked me on my ass, and pushed himself inside of me once more. I took the lead this time, and bounced my hips back and forth against his. He wrapped my hair around his hand, and pulled tight. I arched my back and grabbed my own breast. He sped up and showed me no mercy. After her came, he slowly pulled out of me and rolled over on the mat. He grabbed my hips and pulled me in his direction.

"Well, that's one room christened. We have plenty more to go."

"You are so nasty." We both laughed, but I hopped he was serious, because in five minutes I knew I would be ready.

CHAPTER EIGHT

Courtland

I entered her from behind deeply, and almost nutted right inside of her. Her walls gripped my dick so tightly, that it was almost impossible not to.

"Damn, daddy." She moaned out in ecstasy.

She gripped the back of my leg and pulled me closer to her so that I could go deeper.

I gripped both sides of her hips, and deep stroked her, until I could feel the insides of her get wetter.

She couldn't stop moaning, which meant I was doing my job correctly.

"Ahh—" she tried to scream out.

I hurried and covered her mouth, so that no one could hear us.

"Shut the fuck up, girl." I told her. I was trying to keep quiet myself.

She tried to laugh it off as she tried to push me off of her, but I wasn't done yet.

I gripped the back of her neck and bent her over even further, and began stroking her short but strong, so that she knew I was in complete control.

She moaned in relief when she came all over my dick. I finally nutted inside the condom, and left my throbbing dick inside of her for a moment. She slowly pulled herself up, and I pulled out of her.

I took the condom off, and tied a knot at the top. I shoved it in my pocket quickly, after I pulled my pants up and buckled my belt. I was going to flush it down the toilet when I got back to my office.

"Alright, ma'am." I had already forgotten her name. I watched as she quickly tried to fix her skirt and make herself look presentable again. "Have a good shift." I smacked her on her ass.

"Yes, sir." She whispered. She opened the door to the storage room just enough for her to exit, and silently closed the door.

I looked down at my watch; it was only thirty minutes after noon, which meant business was about to pick up tremendously.

I walked out of the storage room a few moments later.

"Oh, shit!" I was expecting Jenna to be sitting at the bar. It was that she wasn't pleased. Her arms folded across her chest, and her brows were furrowed.

"Courtland, what's your problem?" I could see the irritation all over her face and hear it in her voice.

"What you mean?" I straightened my tie, and close the door behind me.

"We have guests in the building and here you are screwing one of the workers—while she's on duty." She leaned over the bar so that only I could hear her. She was trying to keep her voice as silent as she could.

"Oh." I tried to act like I cared, but I didn't. "I thought she was on break or something." I grabbed a glass to pour me a drink. I didn't like being questioned by my assistant; it felt unethical.

"This isn't a joke. She's the third worker I've had to let go in the past two weeks."

"Wait." I thought about it. "So is that what happened to Angela and Jordyn?" I knew I hadn't seen them in a while. I had been so busy, that I forgot to ask why they hadn't been in.

"Yes, I had to let them go. I don't need the help sleeping with their boss. They start feeling entitled, and I don't need any extra drama, and neither should you." She stared at me so hard, I became uncomfortable.

"Okay, okay, I'll do better." My hands were up in surrender. I was ready for her to move onto her next task. It wasn't her business who I fucked. If I saw something I liked, I had every intention of maximizing all of my options.

"No, you won't sleep with your staff." She looked at me to tell her that I understood.

"Sure, whatever you say, boss." I drank the last of my whiskey and poured myself another glass.

"Look." She stood up from her seat. "I'm serious, and this is getting ridiculous. I'm starting to worry about you. Get it together." She walked out before I could respond, which was probably for the best.

Jenna was a great asset to my company, but I didn't want her too deep in my business. I was a grown ass man, and I could do grown ass man shit, and I was going to need for her to understand that. Hell, Sin hadn't given me more booty in these past couple weeks, and I had needs.

I made a quick stop by my office bathroom to freshen up; I had a meeting with Damien, and I was already late.

I stepped into my private shower, and I could still feel how tight that young pussy was. If Jenna didn't want me sleeping with the staff, maybe she should hire ugly chicks. *Nah.* I quickly dismissed that thought. What kind of money would I bring in with an ugly staff? I laughed to myself.

I finished freshening up, and was out of the Palace in the next twenty minutes.

I jumped in my truck and headed towards the strip club. It had been a long time since I had been to one, and it took a lot of convincing to get Damien to meet me there.

When I made it inside, I felt like I was right at home. I remember when I would go to the strip club at least four times a week. The women were beautiful.

Damien was sitting in a corner in the back. He was eating wings, and had a drink already.

"You had me waiting forever." He was trying to act mad, but we both knew he was enjoying himself.

"Sorry, man, I got caught up."

"Sure." He dismissed my excuse.

"Yeah, but you left me hanging." I was teasing him about ordering without me.

"I was hungry, and you were taking too long. I didn't completely forget you though. I got you a water with lemon to start you off."

"Oh, thanks." I waved my hand at him sarcastically. I watched the girls dance, as I sipped on my water.

"Bruh, what's going on with you?" Damien laughed.

"What you mean?" I'm sure Jenna had already told him what happened earlier today.

"Jenna firing chicks left and right, because you give them executive benefits."

I laughed at his joke. "Yeah, and she needs to stop before I fire her."

"You ain't letting go of Jenna, and you need to stop. You playing with fire messing with all them women that works for you. You know you don't shit where you eat."

"It ain't like this is new to me. It's not like I had never slept with a woman that I worked with before. You could say that Sin worked for me, and I was owning that pussy on a regular basis." I didn't mean to be so vulgar, but I needed him to get my point.

"Yeah, so what's going on with you and Sin? You told me that she was coming through to see the Palace, but you never told me what happened. You should be happy y'all spent some time together."

"She came and we talked. I think she's doing her own thing right now, and wants to get grounded in her new business." I decided to be honest with him. There was no need in trying to front about the situation.

"Oh, so is this why you fucking every chick you see?"

"Nah, I'm just doing what I want." I wasn't fucking every woman I saw. I still had standards and shit. "We didn't really discuss us, so there's no point in trying to force her into something that she doesn't want.

"Cool, but you're not a reckless person, so stop before this catches up to you."

"Nothing is going to catch up to me." I assured him.

"Man, you say that, but I don't want to hear that you got caught up in some mess with chick. Let me be upfront with you now, I ain't listening to you bitch about how you messed up and you want your woman back."

"Alright, alright." There was some truth to what he was saying. I didn't need to get caught up in some shit that I couldn't get out of.

He continued eating his wings. "Did she say she didn't want to be with you?"

"Nah."

"So, how you know she doesn't want to be in a relationship with you?"

"She didn't talk as if she wanted to be back in a relationship with me."

"So what exactly did she say about you all and your relationship?" He looked confused.

"She didn't say much, but she did say that we are going to get through this, so I know she isn't going anywhere. I just know that obviously right now we still have some things we need to work out."

"And that's all that matters to you, huh?"

"Pretty much. One thing I don't have to worry about is Sinaiyah ever leaving me. She loves me too much. We've been through too much shit and overcome too much shit to just be done with each other. She is forever going to be my woman, and I stand my ground on that."

"Oh shit, Courtland!" Damien was being dramatic. I knew he wasn't expecting me to say any of what I had just said. "I hear you, my brother, no need to get hostile." He had a comical expression on his face, which made me laugh at him.

"She's mine, and she ain't going nowhere." I took another sip of my water. I wasn't in the mood to order any food.

"Fucking all them bitches got you real confident these days, huh?"

I stared at him blankly. "You know you not funny, right?"

"Never tried to be. I know what I am, and that's real."

"Yeah, whatever." I continued watching the girls dance.

"How's Viv?" I hadn't talked to her this past week.

"She's great. She wasn't feeling too good this week, so she took some time to recuperate."

"She straight now though, right?" I felt bad that I hadn't checked on her.

"Yeah, man."

"Would you like a dance?" A pretty dancer walked up to our table.

"Why not?" I leaned back in my seat and enjoyed my little dance. I knew Damien was uncomfortable, and that made it all worthwhile.

CHAPTER NINE

Sinaiyah

"I know what I did was unforgiveable, but please give me another chance. I've waited so long for this moment, because you're the one I want."

Landon had been trying to get me to forgive him for the past fifteen minutes, and I still wasn't moved by what he was saying to me. I didn't have any intentions of seeing him again after we last spoke a few weeks ago, but he was not giving up.

"What do you want from me, Landon?" I had to get serious with him. "We have nowhere to pick up from. You don't even know the woman I am today."

"But I want to know who you've become," he pleaded.

"Okay." I took a sip of my sweet tea. I didn't want to argue with him. Clearly, he believed that things would somehow work between us, and I was determined to let him figure out that we had no future on his own.

"Okay?" He was surprised by my answer.

"Yeah, okay. So what's next?"

"Dinner next Tuesday evening." He was grinning so hard; I could see every tooth in his mouth.

"Okay, well I have to get back to the office." I stood up and placed my purse on my shoulder. "Text me the details, and I will meet you."

He stood up from his chair. "I can't pick you up?"

"I would rather you not." I didn't want him knowing where I lived. I had one man who used to think he could pop up on me at any time, and that was enough for a lifetime.

"Okay." He backed off of me, which was smart of him, because I didn't need any pressure on the subject.

I turned around and left the restaurant before he could extend his arms out for a hug. I already felt awkward in his presence, and I wasn't ready for any physical contact.

I walked to my car that was parked on the side of the street and jumped in. I pulled into the street blasting Drake's latest album and headed back to my office.

When I pulled up, I noticed Viviana's truck in the parking lot. She had beaten me to the office, which was fine; I needed to talk to her about a few things.

"Hey, Momma." I walked through the door and my mom was sitting in a chair facing the windows.

"Hey, Baby." She was pulling out art pieces from a box.

"Where are the girls?" I was speaking of Jaslynn and Viviana.

"Throwing out the boxes we've already emptied and broken down. They should be back up in a few, but I want to know how lunch was this time."

"It was fine. I'll give you the details later." I didn't want the motherly advice just yet.

"Okay, well, I can't wait." She started taking the bubble wrap off one of the pieces.

I headed down the hallway, and caught the girls as they were coming back in from the back door.

"Hey, ladies." I was so happy to see them both. They looked great, and seemed to be just as happy to see me.

We all hugged, and Jaslynn caught me up with the progress she'd made on the grand opening.

"Well, I know you got something good for me." Viviana leaned against the wall, and looked me up and down.

"C'mon, silly." I walked past her into my office. She was on my heels ready to hear everything.

"So how did your meeting with Landon go?" Viviana asked as soon as I shut the door. She took a seat in the chair across from my desk.

"It was okay. I hate to bring you into my relationship mess." I sat at my empty desk and dropped my head into my hands.

"Girl, bye." She laughed. "I know we started off rocky, but you should know I have your back."

I laughed, because she was right. She hadn't done anything to hurt me; she had only tried to protect me from the things she could step in about.

"Oh, I know." I took a deep breath. "I just don't think I can trust Landon. It's been too long. I don't know who he is anymore, and I'm not really that interested in finding out. You get what I'm trying to say?"

"Umm, yes! Hell it's been years since you last saw him, and you've blocked all emotions you have for him, but you got to deal with them now. Whether you like it or not, he's here, and he's here for you, so what are you going to do?"

She was right again, but I hadn't really figured out what my plan was exactly.

"Honestly, I'm hoping that he just disappears again."

"Uh-uh." She shook her head from side to side in disapproval. "That's not your best option. He's not going nowhere, so what are you going to do? Don't get any deeper in this mess without a plan."

"What do you think I should do? It sounds to me like you already have a plan."

"I'm happy you asked." We both laughed. "No, for real, I don't have a plan, but I do think you should give him a fair chance, if you do have any love for him left."

"I'm surprised by you." I clutched my necklace.

"Why?" She smiled, even though she had a confused look on her face.

78

"Aren't you supposed to be team Courtland? Y'all are besties. Which is another reason why I hate bringing you into this. I don't want you feeling like you're backstabbing anyone."

"Honey, I'm team happy. You've been through too much to not be happy."

"Awe, you really do care about me." I pushed myself from my desk, and ran over to her, sat in her lap, and gave her a big hug.

"You so unprofessional." She joked with me.

"Shut-up and take my love." I hugged her tighter.

"Listen though, if you don't love him or don't want to open your heart to him again, you should be honest with him, and let him know that you've moved on and aren't interested. No need in stringing him along, and most importantly don't waste your time. You have a lot going for yourself, and your time is valuable."

"Alright, no more preaching." I stood up from her lap. "C'mon, let's finish getting this place together for my brunch!"

We walked back to the front entrance, where my mom was giving orders to Jaslynn on where to put things. I could see the annoyance written all over Jaslynn's face. I felt bad for her. I had given her enough orders on where I wanted things, and how this place should look that she didn't need any extra guidance.

"Mom. Mom." I had to stop her. She was getting on my nerves and I had only heard a couple of seconds of her madness. "I trust Jaslynn's judgment. She didn't help me get this far to have me looking a mess."

"I was only helping." My mom placed both hands on her hips, and I knew it was about to go downhill from here.

Jaslynn kept herself busy; it was obvious that she didn't want any confrontations.

"Leave this for Jaslynn. If she needs you, she'll tell you." I didn't want my mom to mess with Jaslynn's aura. Once I had the vision, I had drilled the vision into Jaslynn, and she hadn't disappointed me yet. I didn't need Mom fussing over nothing.

"Well, hell, she don't need me then!" My mom shouted, she was agitated, and it showed all over her face. "This girl is so organized it's scary." She turned towards Jaslynn. "If I was getting in your way, you should have said something." I didn't approve of my mother's snarky remarks, but I let her get her feelings out. "I will stay out of your way, baby."

"Good." I chimed in so that Jaslynn didn't feel the need to say anything. "Actually," I quickly thought of something for her to do. "I would really appreciate it if you got the break room in order, and our conference area, as well. It would be nice if you wiped down all the furniture."

"Oh, so you want to treat me like the help." She leaned to the side with her hands still on her hips.

"Mommy, please don't do this here and now. Everyone is a part of the help, because we are all trying to help make the grand opening brunch a success."

"Whatever." She pushed past Viviana and I. "Please know," she stopped herself, turned around, and pointed her finger at me, "that I'm only going to clean up because you're allergic to dust."

"Look at you saving my life. You always come through." I couldn't help but be sarcastic.

She rolled her eyes at me and headed down the hall.

My office space wasn't huge, but it was an ample sized space. We had walls installed to give privacy to our clients. I made sure that we designed a room for us to meet in the back, and I, of course, had to give myself a nice sized office. I didn't plan on spending too much time in the office, but I felt I needed one to feel official, and I had every intention to deck it out in fabulousness.

"Are you expecting anyone today, Ms. Sin?" Jaslynn stepped from behind the front desk.

"No." I turned around quickly to see who was approaching my building.

A Black lady with a short cut was walking swiftly to my front door. She was wearing a grey pinstriped suit, and holding an all-black leather messenger bag on her arm.

"Well, let's all keep calm." I looked at Viviana, who looked just as confused.

Jaslynn opened the door once the lady was close enough. "Hello, ma'am, we aren't open for business yet. Can I help you with anything?"

"I'm here to see Ms. Sinaiyah Lockhart. Is she available?"

"For what exactly?" Jaslynn asked.

"I'm Agent Jayda Lang with the Department of Internal Revenue Services."

"Excuse me?" I shouted from where I was standing.

Viviana grabbed my arm to stop me from completely going off on this woman. I didn't want any more mess. My life was finally getting on track, and I liked what I had going.

The lady walked into my building, past Jaslynn. "You must be Ms. Lockhart." She stepped towards me with a pleasant smile on her face.

"Indeed I am, but to what do I owe the pleasure of this visit?"

"Is there somewhere we can speak privately?"

"Here is fine." I stood up straight. "This is my financial advisor, and executive assistant. What seems to be the issue?" I didn't have time to make her feel comfortable. If she was here on business, I was ready to talk business.

"Your spending, actually." She grabbed her bag with both of her hands in front of her.

I was offended. All of my money was legit. I had saved plenty of money while I worked at Perceptions.

This was the first time, since I moved into and decorated my condo, that I was splurging with my purchases.

"What exactly is the problem?" Viviana spoke on my behalf.

"It was brought to our attention that we may need to investigate your using of dollars, and I'm here to legitimize your finances." She was speaking directly to me.

"Legitimize my dollars?" I could feel my heart pounding through my blouse. "I'm not using illegal dollars. All of my money is my money that I saved."

"Then you shouldn't have anything to hide," she said, smiling. "So, do you have somewhere we can continue this conversation?"

"Take her to the conference room." I was speaking to Viviana. She motioned for Agent Lang to follow her to the back. "Jaslynn, lock the front door, and don't let anyone in. Let me know if anyone else comes to the front door, and let my mother know I'm going into a meeting. Don't tell her anything." I stressed to her. "I don't need any unnecessary pressure."

"Sure thing." She turned around to lock the door, and I headed to the back.

I took a deep breath once I made it to the door of the conference room. I had to get myself together, I couldn't lose control in front of this lady any more than I already had.

I opened the door, and Viviana was handing Agent Lang a bottle of water.

"We were just waiting on you." She was already fishing through files.

"Yeah, thank God I brought most of your financial statements with me today." Viviana gave me a look of relief, which made me calm down.

"See." Agent Lang seemed to be excited about this meeting. "This is going to be really easy."

I forced myself to smile at her. This was so hard; I hated to be fake, even in business.

"Make yourself comfortable. I'm certain this will take a while." She didn't take her eyes off of the paperwork Viviana had given her.

I took a seat across from her, and took a sip of water. My nerves were shot.

CHAPTER TEN

Courtland

"Our social media marketing is bringing in a lot of younger clients, and we are already getting asked about private parties and exclusive events." Jenna was standing in my office looking happier than ever.

"Really?" We hadn't been open for long, but you wouldn't know if you walked in. There were always people coming in and using our services. I was really happy.

"Yup! Also, you need to approve this marketing strategy, and look over this investment package I put together for you." Jenna sat a stack of papers on my desk.

I wasn't in any mood to look over anything. I was tired and ready to call it a day. I had been in the office all day, and I needed a drink and some head.

"Yes, ma'am. Will do." I reached for the investment package. Damien thought it would be a good idea to have a packet ready for potential investors. I had enough money to keep my business afloat, but investors were always good to have in your back pocket.

Jenna walked out of my office, and I began looking through the packet. It looked really nice how she had it put together. I really didn't want to send these packets out, but we needed to be ready for anything.

There was a knock on my door. "Come in," I yelled from my office chair. I didn't feel like getting up just yet.

"I can't believe you're still here."

"You always have the worst jokes, Damien." I shook my head from side-to-side.

"You think so?" His face turned serious really quickly.

"What do you want?" I ignored his question.

"Nothing at all. Just seeing what was on your schedule for today."

Damien seemed to be in a great mood. It was like he had just found out he won the lottery, but couldn't tell anyone just yet.

"Anything special going on in your world?" I had to ask. He was acting too weird.

"No, not really. Just blessed, and happy." He was smiling from ear to ear, which was weird, because he never smiled this hard.

"Well, I have to get ready for a lunch date." I hadn't told him about Melanie just yet. I wasn't sure just yet how I felt about her. She wasn't like the other women I had relations with. She was worth something more.

"I knew you wouldn't be here long." He went back to the door. "We'll talk later." He walked out and closed the door behind him.

I couldn't help myself from laughing. Damien was definitely a character. He had opened up a lot since we first started working together, and I was happy he did. He had great ideas, and was very observant so he picked up on things a lot quicker than me sometimes, and I appreciated that about him.

I headed out of the office and to the bistro on the other side of town. The sun was shining bright and the sky was clear. The radio was on, and I listened to Matthew Hanson discuss stocks and savings on Business Talk Radio.

When I pulled up to the bistro, I saw Melanie walking inside. I was surprised that she beat me. I parked on the street, and hoped out of the car to hurry and catch up with her.

Melanie was a former employee of mine, although she had only worked during the weekend of the soft launch of my company, because she had gotten a job as an editor at a well-respected magazine located in Buckhead. She was gorgeous. Her mocha skin looked and felt as soft as velvet, and her eyes always sparkled when I looked at her.

Plus, I was trying to do better and not start any mess at the Palace. Jenna had the staff on lock. If they looked at me with a hint of seduction they were placed on probation. It was funny to me, but Jenna wasn't playing any games. She wanted a stress-free and drama-free workplace, and I respected that, because she was right.

I met her at the table. She was seated outside, still wearing her shades staring down at her phone.

"No need to look busy," I took my seat beside her. She looked up at me and smiled, and she threw her phone in her purse that was hanging on her chair.

"How are you?" Her smile was contagious.

"Good. How are things with you?"

"Fabulous." She took off her shades.

"How's work?" I was interested in hearing more about her new job.

"Work is amazing." I could see that she was full of joy. She was so vibrant it was intoxicating. "It's turning out to be a great decision for me. I was so nervous, but everything is panning out perfectly for me."

"That's really good. I'm happy for you." I hated to see her leave because she was great eye-candy, but she was also smart, so I was happy to see her advancing in her career. Our waitress came and brought us some water to start off with and took our orders.

"Have you all replaced me at work yet?"

"No," I laughed. "We haven't hired more staff, and even when we do, no one can replace you, beautiful." I kissed her softly on the lips.

"So what's on your agenda for today?" She leaned forward on her elbows to listen.

"Nothing serious. Just need to handle some business back at the office. What about you?"

"I have a night of editing ahead of me." She took a deep breath. It showed all over her face that she wasn't looking forward to it.

"I can always come over and help you with it, or you could bring your work to my place." I winked at her and smiled.

"But will we get any work done?"

"That's up to you."

"See, no, sir. I can't lose my job before I get settled in for real." She started laughing and the wind blew her curls into her face. Melanie was an effortless beauty.

"I wouldn't allow that to happen, but you know I got you no matter what." I picked up her hand and kissed the back of it.

Our waitress came out a moment later with our food. I didn't want anything special. I was fine with a grilled chicken sandwich and Melanie was eating cedar-grilled chicken with broccoli and brown rice. I couldn't believe that I was going out on a real date. I had thoroughly enjoyed my life as a bachelor, but I really did enjoy making one woman happy.

"I'm happy to know that you will look out for me if needed." She picked up the conversation exactly where we had left off.

"Of course, what type of man do you take me for?" I asked sarcastically.

"Well, you are a man that is pretty powerful, and that kind of puts you into a category."

"What's that category?" I was curious.

"You already know." She laughed. "You know how men of power are stigmatized as."

"No I don't, I want you to tell me."

"You know most men of power are arrogant, mean, selfish, and womanizers. I don't know why you're acting like you don't know this already."

"Do I make up any of those qualities?"

"Not at all, that's why I'm happy to be here with you today."

"I'm happy you're here with me too, and I'm even happier to know you haven't categorized me as any of those horrible things." I kissed her cheek.

"Naw, you aren't any of those things from what I can see. You've been nothing but a gentleman, and kind, respectful, and most importantly you've shown me that you care about me."

"That's because I do. It's hard to pretend like you care about someone you don't give a damn about."

I wasn't sure what I really wanted from her, but I was willing to let time tell. It was nice to enjoy someone's presence, and have nothing expected but my genuine self.

CHAPTER ELEVEN

Sinaiyah

Today was my big day, and I couldn't be any more excited. I didn't sleep much last night, and I didn't care. Mommy cooked my favorite breakfast foods, pancakes, bacon, sausage, and biscuits, and we sat and drank mimosas, until it was time for us to get dressed and head to the office.

For my event, I decided to wear a floral baby doll dress. I added fuchsia and gold accessories, and fuchsia pumps. I slept in pin curls last night so that my hair would fall perfectly for today. I decided to go all out with my makeup. I did a complete face contour. I looked flawless when I saw myself in the mirror. My mom was just as fly. She wore a coral and black fitted dress, with black pumps, and she had her hair pulled back in a bun. She didn't do much makeup but her skin was always flawless, so she could get away with not wearing foundation.

It was a little after ten when we made it to the office, and my parking lot was filled with company cars and vans already. My brunch wasn't going to start until noon, and Jaslynn was already on it. The tables and chairs were being delivered and set up, flowers were being brought inside, and the caterer was already inside setting up.

"Hey, lady! Everything is looking fabulous," I told Jaslynn. I couldn't believe my eyes. There was a large step and repeat with my logo really big in the center, with other companies that helped sponsor the brunch. Across from it was the selfie station that I couldn't wait to jump in.

"Yay!" Jaslynn came down the hall towards me and greeted my mother and me with hugs. "They are almost done putting the chairs in place, and that's half the battle." She laughed, but I could tell she was worn out. She was in her usual black crop top, leggings, and blue and green Nike shoes.

We walked to the back conference room, where the large conference table had been moved to fit five large tables, and a row of three tables for the food and drinks along the side, which was going to be self-serve.

"Well, the tables are gorgeous." I walked to one of the decorated tables. A light gold tablecloth draped the table with a beautiful lily centerpiece and light pink sprinkles shimmered underneath the centerpiece.

"And I made the glass holders for the centerpieces, the most expensive thing on all of the tables are the flowers." She headed back to the front to grab a few more centerpieces that were ready to be displayed.

"Really?" My mom said when Jaslynn returned. She was flabbergasted.

"Yes, ma'am." Jaslynn answered. She finished setting the rest of the tables, like she was on a mission.

I was happy that Jaslynn knew how to budget, because Agent Lang dug deep into my finances. She had looked through my files for four hours straight that evening, but everything checked out perfectly. I was thankful to Viviana too, because she was just as organized as Jaslynn, and was able to give Agent Lang everything she asked for. I wasn't sure who tipped off the IRS, but they were not going to destroy my company or me.

The plan for today was to have an intimate brunch with about fifty ladies. Afterwards, my head esthetician, Cynthia, and myself would start giving basic facials, and hand spa wraps to about twenty of those ladies. We also had little swag bags with some gifts for them to take home, and a coupon for their first visit.

We finished getting everything set up just in time. Ladies started walking in a little after eleven. Jaslynn had to hurry and change into her dress so that she could direct traffic. She looked so pretty in her all white two-piece crop top skater dress set, with a pretty pink blazer, and matching pink pumps. Her gold accessories complimented her outfit very well.

All of the guests took pictures in front of the step and repeat. Her cousin, Sean, came out to take some professional pictures of the event. I was in awe by how beautiful this event was turning out to be. Everything was running so smoothly. Jaslynn definitely deserved all the recognition. It was obvious that she had learned a lot while under Madam Victoria's tutelage.

All of the ladies were seated in front of me looking absolutely gorgeous in their different styles. Jaslynn sat Viviana, Cynthia, herself, my mother, and myself in the front so that everyone could see us.

I listened as my mother introduced me to my audience. I barely heard a word she was saying. I couldn't stop thinking about how much my life had changed over the past year, and how much of a blessing Jaslynn had been in my life. I never would have known she would become my guardian angel but that's exactly who she was to me, and this event was more than proof.

"I would now like to introduce you to my baby girl, and your Doctor of Beauty, Sinaiyah Lockhart." The room roared with handclaps and praise. I wasn't used to such positive energy coming from young women my age.

I rose slowly from my chair, shaking. Viviana grabbed my hand, and told me to breathe, which made me feel a little better. Once I made it to the small podium, I gripped it tightly to catch my breath.

"Thank you, Mommy." I began, and my guests laughed lightly. I didn't want to speak long, even though I knew I could talk their ears off about beauty tips they could possibly use, and habits they should let go of. I took my time, welcomed them, and looked at every young lady in the room as I started my conversational but informational speech.

I enjoyed standing in front of these ladies talking about my company, as they looked to me for answers and advice.

After I finished my speech, I opened the floor for a quick question and answer portion. An older lady in the very back, near the door raised her hand, and when I pointed to her to hear her question, I saw my father sitting by himself with the biggest, proudest smile on his face. I almost began crying. I just wanted to run up to him and give him a big hug. I had no idea he was coming to my brunch, but I appreciated his support.

I answered the lady's question, and turned it over to Cynthia so that she could begin prepping the ladies who desired a facial.

I took my seat and playfully nudged my mother in the arm. "I didn't know Daddy was coming." I was trying to hold back my tears of joy.

"Why would you know? It would have ruined the surprise." She smiled at me and gave me a big hug. "By the way," she said, turning towards me, "you did really good up there. You're a natural."

I was so excited that I could have screamed.

My attention was brought back to reality when I heard laughter amongst the room. Cynthia was getting ready to start her first facial, and I headed straight to the back to greet my daddy.

"Daddy!" I ran up to him and hugged him tightly. "I didn't know you were coming." I could see he was just as excited as me.

"Of course, I was going to see you launch your first business. You know your Momma has been keeping me updated every step of the way."

"Oh, goodness." I wondered how much she had kept him updated about.

"You seem worried." He looked at me with a sly smile on his face. "Now I wonder what she hasn't kept me updated on."

"So, how long are you going to be in town?" I had to change the subject. Today was going perfectly, and I refused for anything to ruin my day.

"I have to work in the morning, so I'll be heading out after I take you to dinner, if that's okay?"

"Ah, yes, dinner, I would love that." I was too anxious to eat, so dinner with my father would be the perfect ending for today. I was such a daddy's girl. "Okay, let me do a few facials, to keep everything moving."

"Okay, Baby Girl." He kissed me on the forehead.

I was excited to do facials for some of the ladies that came out to the event. They really enjoyed being pampered, and I enjoyed being their beauty doctor.

I was exhausted after all of my guests left. I walked to the front, where Jaslynn was pulling boxes from under her desk. She had already changed back into her leggings and tennis shoes.

"Can you say success?" Jaslynn caught my attention.

"Hell yeah!" I gave her a high five.

"We actually may have to do that again." Viviana brought two centerpieces to the front desk.

"Oh, thank you." Jaslynn grabbed the centerpieces and began putting them in the boxes. "The cleaning crew will be here at six, but I want to get those pieces, and whatever else I can save." She headed to the back to the conference room.

I noticed my father talking to someone outside, which worried me a little. "I'm not expecting anyone this late, so who's outside talking to my dad?" I headed to the door. My dad could handle himself, but I still didn't want him talking to random strangers.

I stepped outside, and wrapped my arms around each other because it was cooler than I expected. The sun was still out, but it was pretty shady where my building was located.

"Hey, Dad." My dad turned around and my heart stopped immediately when I saw Landon standing right behind him.

"Landon?" I didn't expect to see him today.

"Congratulations, Sinaiyah." His smile was as gorgeous as it was when we were younger. I hadn't been paying him any mind for so long, that I didn't realize how handsome he was.

"Thank you." I blushed. Surprisingly, I felt bashful about seeing him here tonight. I almost lost my balance in my heels.

"Well, I'm going to head back inside for a minute." My dad gave me a kiss on the cheek and went back inside.

When I saw the door close behind my father, I turned around, and Landon was standing right in front of me. He grabbed me by my elbows, and I felt a rush of energy soar through my body, warming me up.

"I wasn't expecting to see you tonight." I was trying to stay focused.

"I know."

My heart started racing from his witty response. There was an awkward silence, because I didn't know what to say next.

"All I wanted to do was come here and congratulate you on your amazing accomplishment. That's all." His smile seemed so genuine and sincere.

I smiled back at him and he kissed me before I could pull from his embrace.

He was catching me slipping, and the only reason why I wasn't on my shit was because I was still floating on cloud nine from having such a successful event.

He held me in his arms for a few seconds after kissing me. "I'm looking forward to taking you out Tuesday."

"I'm looking forward to it too." I touched his arms, and took a step back from him. "It was great seeing you tonight."

"I'll see you soon, my Sinaiyah." He placed his hands in his pockets, and watched me walk back into my office.

Viviana was waiting for me once I got inside. She had a smirk on her face, and I knew she wanted the details.

"It's nothing serious." I responded as soon as I locked the door behind me.

"Oh, really?" she asked sarcastically. "That kiss looked like it gave you life."

I didn't want to give her the satisfaction of knowing that she was right, but I couldn't help but look at her and smile.

"Looks like someone is warming up to her first love." She winked at me.

"You know what." I stood across from her so that we could speak privately. "I kind of wish it was Courtland. I remember when he would surprise me like that. He was selfish about me, and I'm just surprised that he didn't he didn't come tonight."

"Well, in his defense he wasn't invited, and he's been busy with the Palace."

"I know, but Landon wasn't invited either, but he still showed up. I like a man that takes intuitive."

"Yeah, I know you do."

"I still have my doubts about him. I still don't know exactly what he does. I know he's a lawyer, but I just haven't heard much about him in the city."

"Hmmm."

"Maybe I'm thinking about it too hard," I shrugged my shoulders, "I don't know."

"I got you, boo, don't worry."

CHAPTER TWELVE

Courtland

I couldn't believe my eyes.

Right in front of me sat Sinaiyah, eating dinner with the enemy. The smile on her face made me nervous, because she looked to be really enjoying herself. I tried to gain my composure as I had my own date for the evening: Melanie.

As badly as I wanted to cancel my reservations, I didn't want to upset Melanie, or look like I wasn't in control. I grabbed her hand, walked her to the door, and opened it for her.

I requested a table towards the back, so that we would be as far away as possible from Sin and her former love. *I wonder if they are having sex.* I knew we weren't together, but she was still my woman.

"Follow me this way." I heard the hostess say, bringing my attention back to my date.

Melanie walked ahead of me and we were seated in a cozy booth in the back. We sat in the center of the booth next to each other.

I couldn't get my mind off Sin. A piece of me wanted her to see me out with Melanie, and the other part of me didn't.

I ordered us a bottle of wine to get Melanie comfortable, after our waitress greeted us.

"So how's business been going?" Melanie was stroking my right arm.

"It's fine, I guess." I looked at her and smiled. "It's a little boring since you aren't there anymore."

She giggled lightly. "Sure it is." She was being sarcastic.

"How are you feeling tonight?"

"I'm feeling great." She looked up to the ceiling and smiled. "How are you feeling?"

"Like the man of the year." I gave her a kiss on the cheek.

Her caramel skin turned red.

When our waitress came back, she poured our glasses, and I ordered our entrees for the evening. This was our first real evening out, and I planned to enjoy myself. We had been to lunch, and I tried to make time to go to different art shows around the city, but we had never sat down for a real evening of dinner and conversation.

"What's on your mind? You seem to be a little distant tonight." She looked at me with concern in her pretty green eyes.

"Babe, I'm fine." I leaned over and gave her another kiss, this time on her lips. Her lips were soft to the touch, so I kissed her again.

She started laughing and pushed me away.

"You denying me kisses?" I pouted.

"Nope, not at all." She leaned into me, and kissed me slowly.

"Yes!" I acted as though I scored a goal.

"You're so silly, hunny." She gave me a sexual side-glance.

I reached under the table, and lifted her dress up, so that I could get to the real prize. She didn't stop me, just stared at me with a lascivious look in her eye. I slid her panties to the side, and I could feel her warm pussy dripping with wetness. She grabbed my arm with both of her hands, and moaned softly. I stroked her pussy with two fingers, as I pushed my fingers deeper inside of her so that I could get them good and wet. I pulled both fingers from her pussy quickly, and placed both fingers in my mouth, "Mmmm." I sucked her juices off my fingers, and she watched me as she bit her lip.

Melanie was turned on. She grabbed my face, and kissed me hard, and my dick jumped. She grabbed my dick, and began stroking it, and I almost lost my breath. "Somebody's just as excited as me."

"Yeah. You can definitely say that." I nodded my head. "You're so sexy." I grabbed her breast, and she gripped my dick harder with her hand.

"Here we go." The waitress caught us both off guard, as she sat both of our entrees down in front of us.

Melanie didn't take her hand off of me.

I thanked the waitress, and turned to Melanie, and kissed her. "Why you must you be so bad?"

"Because being good is no fun." She answered me without missing a beat. She moved her hand, and sat up straight, so that she could begin eating.

The last time I was with her, she had just accepted her position, but now she was in her office doing her thing. We talked about her new editor position, and what her future goals were. It was refreshing to hear her talk about her future vision. She made me feel young all over again. I remember when my goals were only a vision, but know they were a full-blown reality, and that felt even more amazing.

"You want any dessert?" I asked her. We had already finished our entrees, and were almost done with our bottle of wine.

"No thank you," she winked at me. "Do you?"

"That's what you're for." I winked back at her. "I can't wait to finish you."

She laughed softly, and I kissed her one more time.

"I love being spoiled with your kisses," she told me.

I kissed her again, and again, all over her cheek, and lips. Her giggle was light, like a little girl.

We walked out of the restaurant hand in hand, and headed down the street enjoying the breezy Atlanta weather. I had us a suite booked at the W Hotel, and I couldn't wait to get her inside.

"Oh." I looked at Melanie, and her eyes were big with excitement.

"What?" I chuckled in confusion.

"I would love a cupcake right now." She looked up at me.

We were approaching a cupcake shop, so we headed straight inside.

"Welcome to Sassy Treatz." A pretty Caucasian woman greeted us.

"Thank you," I had never seen Melanie this excited about food before.

"I see someone has a sweet tooth." I whispered in her ear.

"Yeah, it's bad too." She replied, and walked up to the counter to see all of the choices.

"What can I get for you today, ma'am?" The lady looked at Melanie.

"I want to try the Double Crunch." She was rocking her hips from side to side.

I was enjoying the view, because her hips were full, just the way I liked them, and her skirt was wrapped tight around her small waist and ample bottom.

"And for you, sir?" The lady broke my attention from Melanie.

"Umm." I walked up to the counter, Melanie was already licking the icing from her cupcake, which was making my dick hard. "I'll take the Apple Caramel Wonder."

"Certainly." She grabbed a cupcake from the back row, and handed it to me. I paid and we headed out the shop.

"I can't believe you have me eating a cupcake in public." I joked with her.

"Nothing wrong with a little pleasure." She took another bite of her cupcake.

"I can't wait to taste you." I licked some of the icing off my cupcake, while looking at her.

"You think you can't wait? Shoot, my panties can tell you that I got you beat." She ate the last of her cupcake.

I finished my cupcake, grabbed her hand, and kissed the back of it.

We headed down the street to where my car was parked, and we headed straight to the hotel.

I wasted no time in getting Melanie completely naked once we made it inside our room. I could stare at her body all night. Her breasts were small, but round, and her nipples looked like they were dipped in caramel. I bent over and placed one of her perky breasts into my mouth, and sucked on it hard, as I grabbed the other breast in my hand, and squeezed it. I could hear her moaning loudly. I picked her up gripping her thighs, and walked her to the bed, and laid her down. I bent over and brought her pussy to my mouth so that I could taste her sweetness. She pulled me closer to her by my neck, as she got wetter. I devoured every drop of her, with no hesitation.

"Oh, my God!" she shouted out in ecstasy.

I crawled on top of her, and grabbed my dick as I took my time entering her. She was so tight, and wet, I had to hold my breath as I stroked her slow but steady. I looked down at her and her green eyes glistened from the night-lights that came through the open window.

"Don't leave me." I was about to pull out, I wanted her on her hands and knees. She pushed me deeper inside of her with both of her hands on my lower back.

"You already know you need to take your position." I smiled at her.

She pouted at me. "But you feel so good, I don't want you to go, not even for a second." She tried grinding herself on me, but she was too exhausted to lift herself.

"Think about how good it's going to feel when you get into position." I pulled up from her. "You better not waste any time." I pulled out quickly, and she exhaled deeply.

She tried to get in position as quick as she could. I placed my hand in the arch of her back, and forced myself inside of her. She leaned over even further, which made her pussy clinch tighter around my dick.

"Whooo!" I shouted out, and smacked her on her ass. I gripped her hips tightly and stroked her until we both came.

"Yay," she said with a slight giggle.

I rolled over to the side of her, and held her close to me. I never thought about being with another woman exclusively, besides Sin, but Melanie was making me second think the possibilities. I loved Sin dearly, but seeing her with Landon tonight hurt me to my core, and I figured now may be a good time to move on.

CHAPTER THIRTEEN

Sinaiyah

I wasn't expecting to end my night with Landon inside of a hotel room, but here we were. I was sitting on a bed, with my arms crossed against my stomach. I wasn't nervous, but anxious. I had never been with Landon before, and I wasn't sure if I was making the right decision. I wasn't upset with him as much. I didn't hate him, so I was trying to make the most of our situation. I wanted to make sure I enjoyed this moment, and be happy, because I refused to have any regrets about this. Plus, I wasn't going to lie to myself and act like I didn't want to see what he was working with, and how he worked it.

I watched him close the curtains halfway, to keep just a glare of the night-lights enter the room. He had already taken off his jacket, and tie. If my eyesight wasn't playing tricks on me, it looked like he had a nice, tight body. I was a sucker for strong arms, and watching him flex his arms was getting me hot.

"What's wrong, my Sinaiyah?" He walked towards me and stopped right in front of me.

I took a deep breath. "Nothing." I said, as I tried to smile. I stood up, and he grabbed me by my waist and pulled me closer to him.

The lights in the room were already dim, and I was thankful, because I was starting to feel nervous. Since I had lost a little weight I was a self-conscious about my body. I was used to having a fuller shape, and the weight lost took pounds off my best asset: my hips.

I felt weird. I hadn't been with anyone besides Courtland, and even that felt like an eternity ago. I was sad to see Courtland in the restaurant with another woman tonight. I wasn't sure if he saw me, but he looked so good. I was missing him, but it was clear that I didn't need to. He was moving on, and I couldn't deny him that.

Landon placed my face in the palms of his hands, bringing my attention back to him. He kissed me slowly and it was a kiss full of passion. He made my heart skip a beat, just from a kiss, and that was a feeling I hadn't felt in a while.

I felt I needed to relax and enjoy my time with Landon. He had been a real gentleman on our date, and in general. Lately, he had been up to all types of surprises. He sent me yellow roses to my job, one day he randomly picked me up for lunch, and on Sunday, he took me out for brunch in the city, and it was beautiful. He had really been trying to step up and show me that he was all about me.

I could feel him unzipping my dress, as he continued to kiss me softly. My skin flushed in nervousness. I kicked off my black pumps, because I felt like I was going to lose my balance at any given moment. I took my eyes off him, and looked down; I couldn't look at him.

He pulled the straps to my satin all black dress down, and I let the dress fall to my ankles. My red thong was soaked in my wetness, and my breasts were sitting straight up since I didn't wear a bra. He looked at my body like it was something to worship. I felt sexy standing in front of him.

He unbuttoned his shirt, and then he unbuckled his pants. His body was amazing. My Landon had really grown up. To me, he looked small in his suits, but behind the clothes he was pure muscle. His body looked as though it had been chiseled for the gods. His abs were tight, and his arms were strong and buff.

My body craved to be intertwined with his. I stepped towards him, and he didn't hesitate to pull me to him. I could feel his massive manhood between his legs, and I was eager to feel him inside of me.

He laid me down on the bed and kissed every inch of me, from the skin underneath my chin to the soles of my feet.

I was smitten by the way he touched me; he was taking his time with me, and that made me feel special. This may have been our first night with each other, but

Landon was making sure it was going to be an unforgettable evening.

He entered me slowly, and I inhaled deeply; he was bigger than I expected. I tried not to tense up, because he was taking his time with me. He looked down at me in infatuation, and I felt like his little lady.

I knew I felt good to him, because he bit his lip as he continuously deep stroked me.

He quickly pulled out, and filled me up with his tongue. I couldn't help but grip the back of his head. His head game was amazing. I could feel his tongue taking laps in my wetness. He slurped me up and I was almost fell into an orgasmic-coma. I came all over his face a moment later, and my body felt relieved.

"You my woman." He climbed back on top of me and I felt him entering me once again. He leaned down and kissed me hard. "I just want you to know." He let me know when he came up for air.

I didn't argue with him, I just continued to enjoy the tune of our rhythmic motion.

He scooped me up in his arms, making sure to stay in me completely. He leaned back on the bed, and positioned me on top of him, and placed his arms behind his head. It was my time to shine, and I refuse to disappoint. I rode his dick, until he came and his dick went limp.

I lifted myself off of him, and licked all of my juices from his dick. His dick took no time to get back up. I continued sucking him, and stroking him at the same time. I knew I had him by his soul, when I licked his balls, and he cursed under his breath.

He rolled me over onto my stomach and entered me from behind. He began pounding me from behind, making my ass jiggle. I felt my body tingling, which meant an orgasm was well on its way. Landon came shortly after me. He rolled off of me, and my body felt sore instantly.

Landon wasn't allowing me to go far, he grabbed me by my waist, and pulled me as close to him as possible. I placed my head on his chest, and I felt safe in his arms. Now, I didn't want the night to end.

I woke up before him, because I had trouble falling asleep. I continued lying with him since the sun hadn't come up yet. I watched him inhale and exhale. He looked so peaceful. His skin was silky smooth, and his lips were soft to the touch. I rolled over to look at the clock and it was six-thirty in the morning.

I wasn't sure how I was feeling about Landon now that we had gone to the next level. There weren't any sparks going off inside of me, but I was happy. Honestly, it was nice to have him back in my life. Although he hadn't given me any real answers to his absence, I think I was ready to move on from it, and handle where we were at this time in our life.

I hated to leave him so early in the morning, but I had to. I got out of bed, and began searching for my thong so that I could get dressed and leave. I slipped into my dress, grabbed my purse and heels, and I kissed him good-bye.

"Don't leave me." His voice was groggy.

"I promise to see you again really soon." I told him before I headed out the door. I couldn't stay with him all day. I had to remember to protect myself, and I didn't need to be falling for him after fucking one time. We had a little history, and even if there was hurt there, that history still counted for something.

The sun was starting to show itself as I pulled out of the hotel parking lot.

I felt like a little girl who had snuck out all night, even though I was a grown woman.

I knew my mother was going to have plenty to say when I got inside. I didn't even know what I was going to say, but she was going to have to understand that I was a grown woman, and was capable of making my own decisions.

When I made it to my building, I took my time making my way to my floor. Although I was grown, I still had a lot of respect for my mother, and I didn't want her to be disappointed in me. I headed to the end of the hall and opened the door to my condo. I could smell breakfast cooking, so I knew my mother was up and moving around, probably cleaning or going through the rest of my cabinets.

"Oh, you're back?" My mom was sitting in my kitchen fully dressed with a smirk on her face. She was such the morning person. She and my grandmother would always wake up at four in the morning like they had somewhere to be.

"Yup," I answered her. "What are you up to?" I met her at the bar, and sat down.

"Nothing. So how was your date with Landon?"

"It was a great date," I responded.

"Clearly." She laughed, and looked back down at the magazine she had been reading.

"So, Mom, how long do you plan to stay in town?" I held my breath. I didn't want her to take it the wrong way.

"You already trying to get rid of me?"

"Mommy, no." I was trying to stay calm.

"I've only been here a couple of weeks."

"Mom." I looked at her like she was silly. "It's been almost three months.

"So you been keeping up with your calendar, I see."

"Forget it, Mommy."

"You just want me gone so you can bring that man in this house."

"Mom, that's not true."

"Well, I had plans on leaving anyway."

"Mom, don't be mad. I just think I can finally stand on my own two feet again, but I appreciate you for everything."

"Sure." She didn't want to hear what I had to say. I could tell she didn't want to leave.

"I mean, Mom, c'mon, you weaned me off of heavy liquor. My kidneys and liver didn't agree to the change, but you got me through. I'm going to always appreciate you for that." She tried to hide her smile, but she couldn't help but laugh at me.

It was weird how close my mother and I had become over these past three months. I didn't want her to leave, but I was used to being on my own, and it was time to depend on myself again. Things were going to come together; I trusted myself enough to believe in me again.

"So now that you've kicked me out, what are you going to do today? I don't' see you trying to rush into work."

"Mom, I don't go to work on Fridays." I shook my head from side to side; I thought she had figured that out.

"I figured we could go out and do some sight-seeing. We haven't really done that since you've been here."

"I guess this is my going away activity."

I leaned my head in my arms on the bar. I knew I was going to hear comments like this for the rest of the day. I wasn't ready.

"Well, don't just lay there. Get up and let's go." She headed to the back to change her clothes. Today was going to be an eventful day. I could already tell.

CHAPTER FOURTEEN
Courtland

"I don't trust that man, Damien." We were sitting in my office catching up on business.

"Why, because he took Sin out?" I wasn't sure if he was being serious, or sarcastic, but either way I was becoming annoyed.

"He hasn't seen Sin in a decade, and now he wants to pick up where they left off." I looked at Damien with a smirk on my face. "Tell me something doesn't sound suspicious about that."

"I get where you're coming from, but he's just a man who wants his girl back, and he isn't letting anyone stop him. Plus, didn't you have your own business to attend to? How was your date?"

"Really, Damien?" My annoyance showed all over my face.

"Hell yeah." He leaned back in the chair. "I'm surprised you're letting him impede on what you had with your woman. I remember a time when you wouldn't have allowed this." He chuckled.

I no longer wanted to have this conversation with him anymore, but I needed a favor from him.

"Would you mind looking into his background for me?"

"Do you really think that's necessary?"

I was growing even more irritated. "I can pay someone else to do it."

"No need to get tense. You know I got your back on this, I'm just thinking about how Sin will feel when she finds out, because women always find out."

"She won't. This is strictly between you and I, and I mean that."

"Well, you know I got you."

"I appreciate it, for real man."

"So how are things with you and Melanie? Or is she old news?"

For a moment, I had forgotten about her. We had plans to go see a movie tonight; I enjoyed her company.

"Fine. Things are fine," I responded.

"Well, I'm happy about that. Honestly, I'm happy you've settled on one woman and not your multiples."

I laughed. He and Jenna had brought so much pressure my way about dating my workers.

"I have to pick her up for a movie later."

"Oh, you two are going on a casual date for once." He joked.

"We like to go out and enjoy each other. It doesn't matter if we do something fancy or not."

"Well, it seems you two are getting serious."

"She's a really sweet girl, and I do like her, but we've both agreed to take it slow."

"You're not used to having a working woman that you can't keep tabs on, huh?"

"I actually have to admit; it is a little aggravating. Her schedule is a little more hectic than I thought. I figured as editor, she sits at a desk and reads all day, but no, she's busy doing so much more. I went to visit her one day, and she was reviewing what pictures would be featured. The photographers don't do that?" We both laughed. "Take today for example, she has an event to go to this morning, but she has the rest of the day for herself."

"You got yourself an ordinary business woman that wears multiple hats. I know about that life."

"Yeah, and Sin is an ordinary business woman now, too."

"Aha! You do miss her." He looked as though he had won the golden ticket.

"I do. She was my lady. We've been through a lot together, and to see her moving on is pissing me off."

"If you want her man, you got to go get her."

"Nah, she's happy, and that's all I really want her to be. I just don't want him to hurt her, and something about him seems shady to me."

"Well, don't think too hard about it. It'll figure itself out. That's one thing I've learned since going from being your assistant to becoming your business partner."

"I know it will. I just don't want anyone to get hurt along the way. We've had enough collateral damage."

"Man, you aren't lying."

I stood up and grabbed my wallet from my desk. "Well, I'm about to go get her. Will you be here for the rest of the day?"

"Yeah, me and Jenna are going to go over some marketing ideas. She wanted to catch me up on some ideas you all discussed."

"Cool, have fun with that, and let me know what you think."

"You got it." He stood up, and headed out the door to his office down the hall from mine.

I went downstairs and snuck out of the back door, taking my time walking around to the front area to my car.

I hopped into my truck and headed down the street.

"Hey, Babe," I said to Melanie through the speakers inside of my car.

"Hey! Where are you?" I could tell she was happy to hear from me.

"I'm on my way to you, are you ready?"

"I will be when you get here," I knew she was smiling by the way she spoke.

"Well, I'll see you shortly, ma'am." I couldn't help but smile, she was like a breath of fresh air.

"I can't wait, sir. See you soon."

"Yes, ma'am." I responded, and waited for her to hang up.

I pulled up to her house fifteen minutes later. She lived in a quiet suburb outside of Atlanta.

I walked up to her door, and rang the doorbell. A moment later she opened the door and she looked amazing as usual. She was wearing a flowing floral dress with a tan blazer, and some sexy, tan heels. Her feet looked edible, they were so pretty.

"Hey, Sexy." She stepped up to me, wrapped her arms around my neck, and gave me a kiss.

"You look beautiful." I made sure to tell her as soon as we came up for air.

She took a step back from me and ran her hands down her hips. "You think so?" She turned around so that I could see the full view of her full hips.

"Why, yes, yes I do." I said while enjoying my view. I pinched her ass, and she flinched like a little girl.

"Stop." She turned around and hit me playfully on my chest. "Look, I'm ready." She stepped back inside and grabbed her clutch from the table nearby.

I walked her to the passenger side of the car and opened the door so that she could get in and get situated.

"I'm so excited about this movie." She rubbed her hands together.

We flipped a coin for action move or romance, and somehow romance won.

"All I know is you better stay up for the entire movie."

"It seems really good. This is going to be a good fall movie. You don't think so?" She turned to me for an answer.

"Of course, I do, Babe." I tried to look sincere.

"Oh, whatever." She laughed.

I was happy to take Melanie to this girlie ass show. I planned to keep her attention on my hands for the entire show anyway.

Traffic was starting to pick up, but we still made it in time.

She didn't want any popcorn just a frozen soda. We opted for a seat way at the top, in the center of the theater. It wasn't crowded inside since it was still an early show.

I wrapped my arm around her when the lights dimmed. I didn't want her to get too deep into this movie. Watching her suck hard on the straw to her frozen drink was making my dick jump.

"Damn, babe, you thirsty?" I slid my free hand up her thigh.

She set her drink down and looked at me. She grabbed my dick through my jeans and gripped it tight. "Yeah, but I need something more." She unzipped my jeans. "Think you can help me?"

I was lost for words. She changed up the game on me and I wasn't ready.

She whipped my dick out and forced it down her cold mouth. Her mouth warmed up instantly around my dick, which made my body tingle. I ran my fingers through her straight, long black hair, as she stroked my dick with her mouth. I pulled my jeans down further so that she could swallow me whole.

Her mouth was amazing. "Shit." I moaned under my breath.

That didn't stop her.

She got even sloppier, and spit was dripping down her mouth. I felt myself getting ready to bust, and she sped up stroking me with her hand and mouth.

I came a second later. She slurped me up along with most of her spit in one suck. She grabbed a napkin from her purse and wiped her hands and mouth.

"Now can you shut up so I can finish watching my movie?" She looked at me with a smirk on her face.

"Anything for you, Babe." I kissed the back of her hand, and leaned back in my chair.

I glanced over at her as she sucked on her straw again. I couldn't wait for part two.

I started to doze off in the movie, because I wasn't sure what was going on. Melanie leaned over to me and began kissing me out of nowhere. I figured it was end of the movie because she was tuned all the way into this movie.

She lifted her dress, and sat on top of me. We were face-to-face, and my dick was getting hard.

"You're full of surprises today." I wasn't sure why she was in such a great mood, but I liked her happy.

"Shhh." She unzipped my pants for a second time, and pulled out my dick. She positioned herself on my dick, and it felt like the perfect fit. I gripped her by her ass, and she rode me slowly. Her walls were so wet I wanted to taste them.

"I'm about to cum."

"Handle your business, Baby." I let her have full control. I wasn't sure what to expect. Melanie began bouncing her ass up and down on my dick, and I almost nutted when she started rolling her hips against mine.

"Okay, Daddy. I'm about to cum." I could feel her wetness fill her walls, and roll down my dick.

She wrapped her arms around my neck, and sat on my dick until it went limp.

"Maybe we should come to the movies more often." I was still in shock.

"Maybe." She shrugged her shoulders.

CHAPTER FIFTEEN

Sinaiyah

My mother left early last Friday morning. It was hard to see her go, and for the first time in my life, I actually missed her.

It was dark in my condo since I hadn't turned on any of the lights. I walked to my window to open my curtains, and my living room and kitchen brightened up instantly. It was beautiful outside, and I couldn't wait to get my day started. I opened the door to my balcony to let some air in my condo, and the temperature was perfect. I absolutely enjoyed fall.

Landon had made plans for us to go to the aquarium, and ride the SkyView Ferris Wheel. I had been wanting to do both of these activities for a while, and never made time to do them, so I was excited about this afternoon. The only thing I didn't want to happen was to see Courtland or his new woman.

Lately, Landon and I were going out a lot. I had also finally let him into my condo. It was weird to have him in my space at first, but I warmed up to it. I enjoyed him, and it was fun catching up and reminiscing about our past.

I settled on wearing some dark jeans, with a pink and royal blue blouse. I couldn't decide if I should wear sandals or my chucks. Even though the sun was out now shining bright, I knew once the sunset, it would be breezy. I stood in my bedroom in front of my long mirror trying to decide: cute or simple? It shouldn't be this hard.

My doorbell rang. It had to be Landon. I decided on my chucks. I hurried and took off my sandal, replacing it with the matching chuck. I grabbed my purse and headed for the door.

"Hello, Beautiful." Landon was standing at my door with a single red rose in his hand. He looked nice in his long sleeve button down and Levi jeans.

"Hi, Handsome." I gave him a hug and he kissed my right cheek.

"I like you in this look." He grabbed my hand and spun me around.

"Oh, my casual chic look?" I laughed.

"If that's what's it called, yeah." He laughed.

"Well, thank you." I was truly smitten with him.

I met him outside my door and locked it. I was super excited about the aquarium, and I was trying to conceal my excitement in front of Landon.

We made it to his car, and he made sure to open my car door and close it for me. Landon drove an all-black Mercedes Benz S-Class with leather and wood-grain interior. I reached over to unlock his door so that he could hop right in.

We pulled out into the sunlight and Landon opened the sunroof. I enjoyed feeling the crisp air in my hair.

"I can tell you're excited about the aquarium." he looked over at me. "No need to try and hide it."

"Really?" I was surprised. "How?"

"You're dancing in your seat and there's no music playing." He reached over and turned on the radio.

I blushed, and slid down in my seat. "You're one for details, I see."

"You act like you didn't know that about me." He smiled. His dimple was so deep in is right cheek, I just wanted to kiss it. I decided to go for it. I leaned over and kissed his cheek. You only live once anyway.

"What did I do to deserve that?" His eyes lit up, which made me feel special.

"Oh, nothing." I gave him a mischievous side-eye.

"Well, what do I have to do to get another one?" he asked with a grin.

"You just keep being you, there is plenty more where that came from."

"So can I get a kiss here?" He pointed to his lips.

"Eyes on the road, Mister."

He looked over at me and pouted, he was so cute. I looked out the window and continued my dance.

"What about now?" he asked me after he pulled into a parking spot.

I leaned over and gave him a kiss on the lips. He could take my breath away with one kiss, and I didn't want to ever lose that feeling.

"Yeah," he shouted out, and I couldn't help but smile hard.

"Stop, Landon."

"Nope. Gimme another one." He took off his seatbelt, leaned over me and gave me a hard sloppy kiss. He was so nasty, but I liked it.

"Eww." I wiped the side of my mouth with my hand. "Let's go."

I opened my door, and waited for him to get out.

It was crowded at the aquarium, which I was expecting for a Saturday afternoon. Seeing all the children with their parents made my heart melt. I couldn't help but think what my life would have been like had I not miscarried my child with Courtland. I tried to regain control over my emotions, because I could feel myself wanting to cry.

"Oh, look!" I pointed over my head.

"I see, my lady, and I have no clue what that was." He looked up in confusion.

"It doesn't matter if we know what it is or not, it's about recognizing the beauty in all of the things around us."

"I think you're beautiful."

I blushed. I felt giddy, like I used to back in the day.

"My lady, I'm so happy you decided to give me a second chance. I really missed you." He pulled me closer to him by my waist and kissed me slowly.

"I'm happy I did, too." I rubbed the back of his neck. Although I didn't miss him, I was happy that he was back in my life.

We took our time walking through the rest of the aquarium. I was really starting to enjoy making new memories with Landon. I was starting to feel like a new woman. I had my career, a pretty decent guy on my arm, and I was joyful. It had taken a while for me to get my life back in order, but it was coming together.

The sun felt good mixed with the cool breeze. Atlanta was popping today. The line for the Ferris wheel was longer than I expected. I guess everyone was taking advantage of the clear skies and beautiful weather.

It was finally our turn to get inside, and all of a sudden I felt nervous.

Landon gave me a quick kiss on the cheek, and we got comfortable inside our ride. We snuggled up close together, as we ate the chocolates Landon bought along with the ride. I felt so safe and secure in his arms. I have my own view of the city, but this experience was like none other. Atlanta was a beautiful city. It was crowded, but beautiful nonetheless.

We stopped once we made it to the top of the ride and I was nervous to look down. Landon turned my face to his, looked me in the eyes, and then watched my lips as I bit them. He was making me even more nervous. He kissed me, wrapping both of his arms around my waist. I wrapped my arms around his neck, and brought him closer to me. I couldn't wait to get him back to my place. This was definitely going to be a moment I would never forget.

We made it back to the ground safely and walked around town before heading back to my condo. We decided to order Chinese and watch movies.

"So you really don't eat eggrolls?" Landon was looking at me like I was really missing out on something.

"No, and I've tried them before. They aren't my thing."

"You have to expand your palette."

"Oh, whatever." I poured us both a glass of lemonade, and we got comfortable on the couch.

I let him choose a movie from Netflix. I was more concerned with eating.

"Law Abiding Citizen!" Landon clapped his hands together. "That's my movie." He happily pressed play.

I actually really liked that movie, so I was happy with his decision.

"So you would defend him in court, wouldn't you?" I was speaking of the lead character from the movie.

Landon turned to me with the most serious expression on his face. "Hell yeah."

"I knew it." I laughed to myself.

"That man is innocent in my eyes."

"I get it. I can't completely disagree with you about that."

"Why not completely?"

"Because he did put innocent people in danger. That's the only reason." I felt like I needed to tread lightly, or Landon was going to take me to court for disagreeing. I stood up, grabbed our empty plates, placed them in the dishwasher, and put the empty cartons in the trash.

"Okay. I'll let you have that."

I took my seat beside him. I was enjoying his company too much to argue, even if it was a friendly argument.

He leaned back and placed his arm around my shoulder. I looked up to him, and he licked my bottom lip. Landon was a straight freak, and I enjoyed every moment.

"You gonna dance for me?" He had a grin on his face.

"Not tonight, but if you in the mood, you can." I was smiling so hard.

Landon got up, while the movie was still playing, and started giving me a nice little strip tease.

He started slow grinding the air, as I lifted his shirt to rub on his abs.

He took off his shirt and unbuckled his pants.

"Whoo! Take it off!" I shouted in support of his strip-tease. He spun around real quick and began vibrating really fast. "My, oh my, you're not new to this."

"Yeah, I'm just trying to give you all I got." He laughed in embarrassment, while rubbing his stomach.

"Keep going, baby. I'm enjoying this."

He rubbed his hands up and down my legs, and stood over me with my legs in between his. "I'm happy you're enjoying yourself, Ms. Lockhart." He continued dancing, and groping me until he was standing in nothing but his boxer briefs.

He lifted me up and pulled my jeans down slowly. He bit my panties, and I got wetter.

"Uh-oh, you're trying to get in trouble." Landon was on his knees ready to pounce.

He slid my panties to the side, and looked up at me and smiled. "Oh you have enjoyed yourself." He yanked me towards him by my legs, and removed my panties. My pussy was on the edge on the couch, and he threw my legs over his shoulders. He dove in head first into my yummy goodness. I could feel him licking me from front all the way to back, and I couldn't deny how good it felt.

I moaned his name. He lifted his head, and his mouth was drenched with my juices.

"Did you need anything?" He was being a smart-ass, but I didn't mind. He knew what he was doing. I needed him to finish, but he had me yearning for his tongue. "Didn't you call my name?" He asked. I think he enjoyed me feigning for him. "Okay, well I'm going to finish what I'm doing here, and I'll be with you momentarily." I laughed in pleasure once I felt his thick tongue up against my clit. He sucked hard like it was a jolly rancher. I could feel myself coming all over again and I enjoyed it.

Landon stood up and pulled his briefs down. I hungrily swallowed his dick. I looked like I was bobbing for apples the way I was going up and down his dick. I spit on his dick to make sure it stayed wet and massaged his balls. I smacked his dick against my tongue as the pre-cum flowed from him.

"Damn, girl." He spun me around for me to get on my hands and knees, and I submitted to his dick as he slowly pushed himself inside of me. We started slowly and eased into our own rhythmic flow. Feeling him inside me was making me weak. I leaned over until my breasts were on the floor, and my ass was sticking straight up. This position made Landon speed up. He pulled out when he came.

He rolled me over, and stuck himself back into me. I was surprised that he was still hard. He caressed my breasts as he continued to stroke me. He leaned down, placed one of my hard nipples in his mouth, and played with my nipple piercing with his tongue. He came up and kissed me hard. He lifted my right leg and placed it against his chest, while my other leg stayed put near the floor. He was about to nut, and I was about to cum all over again.

We came hard together, and it felt so good. I knew we were both about to get the best sleep ever. We were breathing so hard I knew neither one of us were going to get up. I reached for the throws that stayed on my sofa, and covered us with them. I turned off the television, and snuggled up under him. We were good right here on the floor.

CHAPTER SIXTEEN

Courtland

"I can't tell her this shit, man." I laid my head back on the sofa. My head started throbbing thinking about what I had just read.

"You sure as hell can't." Damien had a disappointed look on his face.

"Man, are you absolutely sure?" I sat back up straight on the sofa.

"Oh, yeah."

I didn't know why I asked if he was sure. I knew he was sure. Damien always double checked. We were sitting in Viviana's living room trying to keep our voices down so that she couldn't hear us from upstairs.

"Have you told Viviana?"

"Of course not! You said this was strictly between us." He looked at me like he was ready to attack me. "Trust me. I wanted to tell her, but I am a man of my word."

"I know. I know, but I may need her." I knew he wasn't going to approve of me wanting to bring her into this situation, but I was going to need her.

"For what? I don't want her involved in any foolishness." His voice was firm.

"I know." I rested my face in my hands. Her help in this situation would be greatly appreciated. She was the only one who would be able to talk to Sin about this.

"When was the last time you spoke to Sin?" I could see him trying to piece a plan together in his head.

"It's been so long, that I'm not even sure."

"You need to leave this one alone, it would turn into a messy situation quickly if you got involved."

I sat there contemplating if I should or shouldn't get involved and if I should or shouldn't get Viv involved. Damien had found some information that would ultimately hurt Sin, and I knew I didn't want my name tied to any part of it. I had caused her enough pain, and the last thing I wanted to do was hurt Sin again. She was getting back on her feet perfectly without me, which hurt me to watch, but I was happy for her.

"Don't do anything you would regret." Damien snapped his fingers bringing my attention back to our conversation.

I turned to look at him. "Viviana has to let her know." I stood up and headed upstairs. My hands were tied, but she could have this conversation with Sin woman to woman.

"Courtland, leave her out of this!" Damien was on my heels. He pulled me back down two steps, and I almost lost my balance. Damien scowled at me, and I knew he would fight if I brought his woman into this mess, but I had to take a risk.

"What is going on?" Viviana came walking out of her office after hearing our little scuffle.

"I need your help." I uttered.

"Okay, with what?" She folded her arms across her chest.

"No, he doesn't." Damien interjected, and looked at me with an evil eye.

"Look, you gotta tell Sin that—"

"There is nothing to tell." Damien cut me off.

"Now, I'm interested. Let him finish, Damien." Viv walked to the stair rail and leaned over it so that she could see me.

"I don't want you involved in this." Damien met her at the top of the stairs. I could tell he wanted to protect his woman, and I wanted to do the same for my woman. Sin didn't deserve to be brought into any more drama.

She looked at him with a confused look, and looked back at me. "Go ahead, Courtland."

"Donny is married." I blurted out. I didn't have any more time to waste, and the way Damien was interjecting we would be there all night trying to have this conversation.

"And by Donny, you mean Landon." She looked at me for confirmation. I couldn't believe she was so calm. I expected her to shout at me, but she remained composed

"Yeah." I sighed deeply. It was already hurting me to know this information.

"And, I guess, Damien found this information out." She looked at him to confirm.

"Yeah, Baby." He looked down at me with anger in his eyes. "I knew you shouldn't have come here. I knew it." Damien was angry.

She grabbed Damien's hands to calm him down. "Who's the lady?"

Damien didn't want to answer her. She gave him an evil glare.

"Her name is Heather-Nicole Jones," Damien answered.

"Do you know where she works or a home address?"

"I don't want you caught up in any love triangle," Damien pleaded with her.

"I can assure you that won't happen, but I need to talk to her. Give me her information." She walked past Damien and headed down stairs towards me.

"Viviana, do not get involved in this," Damien warned her. "Matter of fact, I don't want you involved in this."

She walked past me, and I followed her into the kitchen. I was so thankful that she was willing to help me, but I couldn't help but wonder what she was thinking.

"So, I guess you want me tell Sin about this, Courtland?" Her voice sounded very sad.

"I hate to ask." I was being honest, I didn't want Viv cleaning up my mess, but I knew it wouldn't be well received coming from me.

"No, you don't. Give me her information, Damien," she shouted. Viv seemed like she was starting to get frustrated with Damien.

Damien walked into the living room, leaving Viviana and me in the kitchen.

"I appreciate you doing this for me."

"Let me stop you right there." She held her hand up to my face. "I'm not doing this for you. I'm doing this for Sinaiyah. She's been through enough and if I can stop her from being hurt by a man who is clearly the scum of the earth, I will." She reached in the cabinet to grab herself a glass.

I wasn't sure how close Viviana and Sinaiyah had become, but from how Viviana spoke, they had to be really close. I could tell that she really cared about Sin, and that made me smile. Sin deserved a genuine friend like Viv.

"Here you go." Damien walked back into the kitchen and handed her some papers.

"What made you look into this?" She asked Damien.

"Courtland asked me to look into it after he saw them on a date. He didn't trust the guy." He shrugged his shoulders.

Viv went to the refrigerator and pulled out a pitcher of sweet tea. "So how long has he been married?"

"A while." Damien took a deep breath. "The brother has been married long enough to have two kids with her, ages three and one."

I shook my head from side to side. Donny had some nerve to try and run game on my woman.

"Honestly, Courtland had every reason to not trust that man. It wasn't easy to find a copy of his marriage license. It was sealed for some reason. With most marriage licenses, it'll come up in the system automatically, but I had to do some serious digging for this." He finished explaining himself. "At first, I thought it was something that was expunged, like he had a criminal past, but no, it was his marriage license. He has to be very well connected to be able to hide something like this. If he can hide this, I wouldn't be surprised what else he could be hiding. It's definitely a red flag."

"You didn't find out?" Viv seemed upset with him for not doing a thorough search.

"This was enough evidence to me for what Courtland asked me for."

"Oh okay, I get you." Viv looked at me with sad eyes. "Courtland, this is horrible."

"I know. That's why she has to know, and you have to tell her."

"You're right." She took a sip of her tea. "And you're right to stay out of it. Don't get any deeper in this than you need to. Knowing Sin, she's gonna need you. You've been her anchor for so long, that I can only imagine you'll be who she runs to when I tell her. So

140

please don't do or say anything crazy, and please act like you don't know." Viv shook her head from side to side. I noticed that she looked exhausted.

"I most definitely will. Viv, I really do appreciate it." I walked up to her and gave her a hug.

"I know you do. Courtland, I know you never stopped loving her, just like she never stopped loving you."

Hearing Viv say that made me feel good, because she was right. I couldn't wait to be Sin's anchor again.

"Thanks again." I gave her another hug and she hugged me back.

"I got it from here, fellas, if I need you, I'll let you know." She grabbed her glass and headed back upstairs.

"I don't know about this." Damien started again, this time with just me.

"Damien come here, and Courtland, you can go." She yelled from upstairs.

Damien gave me a side glare, and headed to the door to let me out.

"I'm sorry, man, but I need her help." I grabbed my jacket and walked out the front door.

"Yeah, whatever, I know. Anything for your lady." He closed the front door.

I walked back to my truck, and I felt an overwhelming sense of sorrow for Sin. I didn't want her to get hurt, and I was starting to regret bringing Viviana into this mess. I didn't want this to backfire on anyone.

CHAPTER SEVENTEEN

Sinaiyah

I was sitting in my car listening to Beyoncé's Flawless. I needed a quick confidence boost. This day couldn't come fast enough. I could still remember the day Viviana had come to me with some information she found on Landon. I remember telling her that I wanted to know a little bit more about him at my brunch, but I wasn't expecting her to find his entire family tree, including his wife.

I was happy to have a friend like Viviana looking out for me. She didn't want this to turn into a scandal, being that I was branding myself into a positive image despite my negative past with Perceptions and its downfall.

Viviana decided to have a meeting at her office with me and Landon's wife, Heather-Nicole. Thankfully, she was willing to talk to me, and clear up any questions and concerns I had, which I really didn't have any.

I was starting to have second thoughts about going into this meeting. I didn't want to meet his wife, but a part of me needed to see her so that I knew it was real, and that he wasn't worth shit. I was sitting in my car trying to waste time parked outside of Viviana's office. I couldn't shake my nerves, not even with Beyoncé playing through my speakers.

I had finally let my guard down with Landon, and could feel myself starting to love him again, and I didn't want to lose this feeling. Things had been going perfectly between us. I couldn't believe that he would hide a whole life from me. I didn't want to believe it was true.

I turned off my car and jumped out before I changed my mind. It was getting late and the clouds were getting darker.

I walked up to the front door and pulled it open. The door chimed, and I could hear Viviana in her office in the back. I could feel a nervous rush through my body. I wasn't sure what to expect when I made it to her office. I was hoping this was a joke by some horrible friends.

"Hey, Sinaiyah." Viviana came out of her office, startling me.

"Hey." I gave her a hug to get rid of my nervousness.

"Don't look so alarmed." She began whispering to me. "She is just as nervous, with a hint of anger, but we are going to keep this light. Remember what I told you earlier. You're the victim, she knows this, and doesn't blame you for anything. She just wants to address the situation so that she can know how to move forward."

She grabbed my hand and pulled me into her office before I could digest everything she had just said.

"Heather-Nicole, this is Sinaiyah. I hate that you two have to meet like this, but I think it's best we do this in a private environment where everyone feels safe and can talk freely."

Heather-Nicole rose from her seat and stood face-to-face with me so that we were staring at each other. We looked each other over, as if sizing up competition.

Heather-Nicole was a pretty chick. She looked mixed with her curly brown hair and dark brown eyes. She didn't have a bad figure either, for her to be so petite. She had a nose piercing that made her look eccentric, and the glitter eye shadow enhanced that look.

"Well, I'm his wife." She clasped both of her hands together as she spoke in a defensive tone.

"And I'm his first love." I responded, with a smile on my face. I was okay with coming together for a civilized conversation, but I refused to be disrespected on any level.

"Alright, ladies, let's have a seat." Viviana walked around to her desk.

I pulled out the chair that was meant for me, closer to the door. We were already off to a rough start, and I didn't want to have to put this chick in her place if she got out of line, even though I was prepared to do so if necessary.

I placed my purse in my lap and waited for what was next. I was starting to feel like this was childish and unnecessary. I felt like a sorority girl coming together with her sister for a lemon squeeze because somebody's feelings were hurt.

"So how long have you been seeing my husband?" She crossed her legs, and turned in my direction.

"Do you want me to start from the beginning when we were both in high school? Or would you rather me start with the most recent?" I responded with the same amount of attitude she asked me with.

"Did he tell you about our kids?"

She cut me deep with that. I tried to remain calm, but I knew my disgust showed all over my face. It was one thing to have a wife, but to have a wife and an entire family with her was too much. "If he didn't tell me about you, what makes you think he acknowledged your kids?" It was clear she was trying to hurt me, so I had to respond with the same amount of hurt.

"Okay, this isn't going anywhere." Viviana stood up and walked around her desk, and stood between us. "If you both are going to attack each other we can all leave with no resolution." Viviana leaned back on her desk.

"This is unnecessary." Heather-Nicole grabbed her purse from the floor, and stood up from her chair.

"Listen, listen." Viviana interjected. "Remember that you both agreed to be here."

"He's never acknowledged you to me." I spoke in an apologetic tone. I wasn't trying to hurt her.

"Did you ever ask?" She looked like she was trying to understand. The hate that once showed on her face was gone. I could only imagine how she was feeling. My feelings were hurt after only a couple of months of dating, so I knew she was devastated.

"Well, that doesn't matter because he never gave me any indication that he was married after he went out of his way to find me." She needed to be reminded that her husband wanted me. Finding out about a wife and children caught me off guard. I never felt the need to ask Landon about a wife because I assumed that he didn't have any real baggage. He had chased me down, even though I had moved on without him. I wasn't trying to make him a part of my life, it was him trying to be in mine.

"Wow, so he found you?" She seemed surprised.

"Yes," I pleaded for her to understand. "I did not go after your husband. We grew up together. We were supposed to move to Atlanta together years ago, but he didn't come. After I didn't hear from him, I moved on. That was the only thing I could do." I was being as sincere as I could. "I would never intentionally go after a married man. He found me, and I was in no way looking for him. Honestly, I didn't want to give him a second chance, but he begged me to."

I could see the tears getting ready to escape her eyes. I wanted to hug her, but that wasn't my place. I knew she was hurting. After all the hurt I endured over the past year and a half, I knew what it looked and felt like, and I hated that I was causing another woman to hurt.

"Damn." She hurried to wipe a tear from her eye before it fell.

"Look, I'm really sorry," I told her and I meant it.

"Clearly, this ain't your fault. It just hurts because this isn't the first time he's cheated on me."

"Wait a damn minute!" I was heated. I leaned back in my seat to catch my breath. I wasn't surprised. I quickly remembered that he had gone on a few dates with my ex-best friend, Illeanna. I decided it was best to withhold that information from her. The only reason I didn't hold that against Landon was because he and Courtland both said that it was only a few dates, but who really knew?

"No need to fret over me." She tried to laugh it off. "He isn't happy with me." There was a moment of silence. "I'm tired of feeling like I'm not good enough." She wiped her eyes, and Viviana handed her a Kleenex tissue. "Maybe I'm not pretty enough. Maybe I don't have enough education for him. I don't know, but I'm tired."

I sat in my chair with my mouth hanging open. I hated that she felt this way, because she wasn't ugly. I didn't know how much education she had, and it didn't matter, because from the way she spoke, it was clear that she had enough intellect to get her by.

"Stop talking like that. It doesn't matter if you're ugly and dumb, or fine and educated. The fact of the matter is he chose you and made a commitment to you. He needs to stand by you."

She looked at me like she was thankful. Her eyes were blood shot, and her nose and cheeks were flushed.

"Thank you." She cried into the tissue. She was trying to get herself together.

Viviana, embraced her like they had been friends forever, and I was happy she did. I didn't know if she had any real girlfriends, but it was clear that she needed to be loved on.

"I have to go." I was getting emotional, and here wasn't the place for me to cry. "Heather-Nicole, I'm going to call you later this week. Stay strong, and don't do anything drastic, okay? Don't even mention to him that you know about me." I looked at her to make sure she understood me. She nodded her head in approval. "When you see him, act like you're not on to anything that he's doing, be sweet and extra loving. I assure you, we're gonna get his ass, and I mean that." I almost cried talking to her.

I was pissed off. Landon had come back into my life, and played me. Neither Heather-Nicole or me deserved to be treated with so much disrespect.

I didn't need him in my life, and I was ready to fuck up his entire world.

CHAPTER EIGHTEEN

Courtland

I had already missed three of Sin's calls. I didn't want to be rude, but I was sitting at dinner with Melanie trying to listen to her talk about an event she was heading to after we finished dinner.

"Answer the phone, Courtland." Melanie was clearly agitated.

"You're my only focus for the evening." I tried to reassure her.

"No, I'm not. It's tearing you up that you haven't answered her call." I could see her trying to hide her disappointment.

"Babe, please don't be upset." There was no point in lying. I had to have been wearing my emotions all over my face, because I hated that I couldn't answer my phone. Sin hadn't blown up my phone in a while, so to know that she needed me and I couldn't be there made me feel bad.

"Just see what she wants so that we can finish enjoying our evening." That made her smile a little and she continued eating.

That's not what she really wanted me to do. I knew she was just being nice. I ignored the call again, and my phone buzzed a second afterwards, indicating that Sin left a voicemail.

"So finish telling me about this event you have to leave me to attend this evening."

"Don't do that." She smiled. "I don't want to mix my business with my pleasure." She smirked. And since we have decided to take things slow and not rush into a relationship, I think it's best if I attend this event alone.

"Uh-huh." I gave her a sly smile and licked my lips. "I get what you are saying to me." I nodded my head up and down.

"Don't be mad at me." She frowned a little and poked her lips out.

"I get it. You're still new, and you don't need everybody assessing your love life."

"You do get it." She looked shocked. "I didn't want you to get the wrong idea. I don't want you to think you're my little secret. I'm just protective over what we have. I enjoy our time together and I don't want to bring you around prematurely. You know?"

"Yes, ma'am, I do." I leaned over and gave her a kiss on the lips. I wasn't upset; she had a job that had her occasionally in the limelight, and in that industry, sometimes less is more.

"Thank you for understanding." She pushed her lips out for another kiss, and I couldn't help but give her another one.

We finished our dinner and I walked Melanie to her car so that she could head to her event.

I called Sin back as soon as I got in my truck.

"Hey, you straight?" I asked as soon as she answered the phone.

"No." I could hear her crying.

"Where are you?" My body felt tense. I didn't like knowing that something was wrong, but I was happy to know that she called me.

"I'm…" Her voice trailed off. She was crying uncontrollably. "I'm…home."

"I'm on my way. Don't hang up." I kept her on the phone, and listened to her cry over the phone.

I wasn't sure if Viv had just told her about Donny's wife and family, but I wanted to be there for her. I hadn't spoken to Viv in about a week, and Damien didn't want to discuss the situation.

It didn't take me long to pull into the parking lot and take the elevator to her floor. I ran down the hall and looked through my key ring for the key to her door. I walked through the door and it was pitch black inside. I could hear Sin in the living room, sniffling. I walked towards the sounds, trying to feel my way around, and Sin was lying on the floor wrapped in a blanket, with one candle burning on the other side of the room.

"Babe, what's wrong?" I was trying to treat this situation delicately. I didn't want to assume that I knew what was wrong, or give any hints that I knew about Donny just in case she didn't know yet.

I took my jacket off, along with my shoes. She didn't move. I crawled down to the floor, and held her tightly in my arms. Her hair was all over the place, and she couldn't look at me.

"Sin, look at me." I rubbed her back, so that she would feel safe. "Look at me, Babe." She wiped her eyes and looked up at me. Her eyes were all I could see and they were swollen and red. She had the blanket pulled to her nose and she looked past me to the other side of the room. "What happened?" I didn't take my eyes off of her.

"I shouldn't tell you, but I need you right now." Her voice was above a whisper.

"I'm here." I pulled her closer.

"So, I decided to give Landon a chance to prove himself to me." She sniffled. "And things were actually going great—perfectly, you could say." She finally looked me in the eyes.

I continued listening even though I already knew for sure where this was going. I wasn't sure what Viv's plan was or how she decided to bring this information to Sin, but I knew she handled her with care. I knew Sin would be hurt, but I wasn't expecting her to be this devastated; Sin was a strong girl, but maybe she still had feelings for him.

"He's married, Courtland," she yelled out and tears ran down her face. "That man is married." She pushed me away from her. "Oh, but wait, there's more." She took her arms out of the blanket, and a look of anger

154

came over her face. "He's married with children. Yup, he's got kids." She tried to laugh it off, but it was more than obvious that she was hurt.

"I got you, Babe." She laid her head on my chest, and began crying all over again. She reached out and wrapped her arms around my neck. I didn't understand how he could have an entire family and turn his back on them the way he did. I was furious just from knowing that he was married to another woman, but I knew not to put anything past him after he manipulated me and a few others to get to Sin.

"You know what hurts most?" She raised her head up and looked at me.

"What?" I was trying to hide my own anger and listen to her.

"He came back into my life. I was fine without him. He hurt so many people to get to me, and I had no intention of giving him any attention, until he begged me." She looked astonished. "Although I don't agree with him hurting you and Illeanna to get to me, I never expected him to hurt me." She unwrapped herself completely from the blanket and laid her head in her hand. "I sound crazy." Her brows rose up. "Of course he would hurt me. He's selfish, and would do anything and hurt anyone to make him happy."

"Don't think about it, Babe." I wanted her to get all of her thoughts out, but she didn't need to give this situation more energy than needed. To see her hurting over some blast from the past made my blood boil. Viv was right when she called him the scum of the earth.

"C'mon, Courtland, you know I can't."

Her eyes were still red, as she tried to hold back her tears.

"You know you've been through worst, right?" I tried to put a smile on her face.

"Oh, God!" She rolled her eyes, and tears began to fall.

I wiped them away and smiled at her. "So you know this will be water under the bridge really soon?"

"Yeah, but don't you do anything. I know how you get down." Her face was serious. "Trust me when I say he has it coming."

"Oh, really?" I was surprised to hear her say that.

"Yeah." Her eyes brightened up instantly, the way I liked to see them. "Thank you for coming tonight, Courtland. I appreciate you so much for this."

"Anything for you, Babe." We kissed and I was in disbelief.

"Oh, my goodness." She sat up in complete embarrassment, "I'm so sorry, I didn't mean to. I mean, I know you have a girlfriend. Oh, God, I'm so sorry!"

I didn't know she knew anything about Melanie, maybe Viv told her, but I brushed it off. I pulled her back down to me. "No, I don't have a girlfriend, but I am seeing someone. But don't you ever be sorry for kissing me." I tilted her chin up and kissed her slowly.

I had missed her lips for a while now, and I didn't want to stop.

"No, I don't want to come in between you and your new lady." She tried pushing away from me, but I held her tighter.

"I'm not letting you go." And I meant exactly what I said.

"I don't want you to." She wrapped her arms around me and kissed me.

I rolled her over on her back, and kissed her neck down to her breasts. They were still as nice and perky through her shirt. She wasn't wearing a bra. I quickly took her shirt off and looked at her breasts staring straight at me; I sucked the life out of them as she jerked me closer. I tugged at her nipple piercings, making her moan my name aloud, and arch her back. I pulled her pants down along with her panties, and removed them from her legs. I lifted her up by her thighs and brought her pussy to my face. I had missed her smell and taste, as I devoured her. She gripped the back of my head tight, as I slurped her up. I licked her clit backwards and forwards, catching all of her juices as they flowed. She started to push me away as I started making circles around her clit. Hearing her moan in pleasure made my dick get harder. I stroked my dick, and slurped up more of her juices. I came up, and my mouth was dripping with her juices. I looked down at her biting her lip like she wanted more. She gasped when I entered her, filling her up with my dick. I felt her scratch my lower back, and I began slow stroking her, breaking down her slippery walls slowly, but surely. I leaned down and kissed her, and she licked all of her juices from my lips and chin. I missed being inside of her, and it felt so good to be back home.

CHAPTER NINETEEN

Sinaiyah

"Whatever you do, please don't sleep with him."

I was sitting in Viviana's office catching her up on where I stood with Courtland. I had been hiding it from her for almost a week now, and I couldn't hide it anymore. Where there was once distance between Courtland and I was now filled with our love. It was liked we picked up exactly where we left off. That scared me, because I was still in a weak space, because Landon and I too had picked up from where we left off.

I scrunched my nose up at her, because Courtland and I did have sex, and it was good!

"You did not!" Her eyes got big. "Please, tell me you did not." She shook her head from side-to-side.

"I mean, I still love him." I was attempting to explain myself, but I knew I was making it worse. I didn't understand why she disapproved so much.

"Isn't he in a relationship?" Her mouth was hanging open waiting for an answer.

"No, but he is seeing a young lady."

"And you're okay with this?"

"Well, at least Courtland isn't married. Plus, I was seeing someone, and still am, until I figure things out."

"Wait, you're still seeing Landon? The married man with a family?" She said to remind me.

"Look, I got this." I didn't need her coming down on me.

"You sure? Because it sounds like you're about to go down a dark and lonely path."

"I'm not." I appreciated her concern, but I knew I had a grip on what was happening.

"I think Courtland is in a relationship with that girl."

My phone started ringing. I looked down and it was Courtland; I declined the call.

"That was him wasn't it?" She laughed. "I can see it all over your face."

"Don't be mad."

"Girl, bye. The last thing I am is mad. I just don't want you to be hurt. I don't know how deep Courtland is with this chick, and we are already dealing with one trauma. I don't need Courtland to be another one, again. We can't forget that he has a track record for hurting you, and I'm not trying to be messy or anything. I'm just trying to look out for you."

Viviana looked so sincere when she was talking to me, and she was right. Courtland had hurt me in the past. I don't think it was ever intentional, but he did have a way of hurting me, and my soul was already weak for him, and from this situation with Landon. I just wanted my old thing back with Courtland. I missed him, and he had never left when times got hard. I mean, he was the one I called when another man hurt me. It's funny how life works. I was lying on my living room floor crying over a man that hurt me to a man who had hurt me previously.

"So are you going to find out how serious Courtland is with that chick?" I couldn't help but ask.

"Uh-uh, don't have me out here doing your dirty work."

"You're already on a roll. You found out that Landon was married and shit. Finding out if Courtland is serious with another woman is light work for you."

She stared at me with a smirk on her face. "You already know I'm on it."

We both laughed.

"Great! I have to get back to work." I grabbed my purse and walked around her desk to give her a hug.

"Thanks for bringing me lunch, my dear." She stood up and gave me a hug.

"Of course, you know I have to keep you fed." I rubbed her growing belly. She was only three months and was barely showing, but I was already in love. She and Damien had decided to keep it to themselves for the first trimester. Viviana was so nervous about having a miscarriage, because she had a few complications, but now she was doing well, and I was excited about becoming an auntie.

"You're right, and we are full." She laughed. We walked to the front door, and I left her to finish her own business.

It was only three o'clock. I had taken a late lunch, because we were crazy busy at the office, which was a great thing.

"Hey you called?" I called Courtland back as soon as I got situated in my car.

"Yeah, Babe. Just checking on you."

The fact that he cared enough to check in on me, made me smile. I missed the caring, sweet, take initiative man he was to me. "Yeah. I'm heading back to work, just finished eating lunch with Viviana."

"Oh, how was that?"

"Fun, I wanted to look over some things with her."

"How is business?"

"It's going great! We are busy, and I'm really happy that my little baby is thriving."

"Me too. I'm really proud of you." I heard a hint of excitement in his voice.

It was nice to hear him compliment me. I always figured we would be some elite power couple running Atlanta, but it didn't work out that way for us, and I was trying to be okay with where we were now, even though I still wanted us to be that power couple.

"How's everything on your end?"

"Awesome. You know that's how it always is for me."

"That's good to hear." I was enjoying having my man back around, even though we weren't official.

"Yeah, but you let me know if you need anything."

I could hear the sincerity in his voice. Yes, sir, and thank you for being here for me." We got off the phone a moment later.

I headed back to my office. Atlanta was busy as usual. The traffic seemed horrible today, but I made it back to my side of town in twenty minutes. My parking lot had dwindled down a lot since I had left for lunch. I was ready to close up for the day and get home to have a glass of wine.

I walked into my building, and the last person I wanted to see was sitting down in my waiting area: Agent Lang.

"Agent Lang, you're back." I wasn't happy to see her, but I put on my fakest smile.

"Yes, ma'am, it's been brought to our attention that we need to check the growth of your company." She jumped straight into business, which really surprised me. I guess she was still mad at how I first responded to her when she came to my office.

"Why?"

"Well apparently, you're bringing in a lot more money than you've accounted for."

I was glad no one was sitting in the waiting area. My customers didn't need to know what was going on.

"And who brought this to your attention?" I was getting sick of whoever kept bringing my company to her attention.

"Ms. Lockhart, you know that is confidential information."

"Agent Lang, please leave." I didn't want to do this during my office hours, even though I was closing in the next hour.

"Now, you know I can't do that, Ms. Lockhart."

I took a deep breath. I didn't understand why she kept coming to my office unannounced. I wasn't going got let her scare me or intimidate my business.

"Let me call Viviana. you can follow me." I walked her to the conference room where we last met.

I was going to have to call somebody and figure out how legal it was for Agent Lang to continuously pop up at my office. I paid my taxes on time and Viviana kept great records of all of my finances, so I didn't know why my company was under attack with the IRS.

Viviana made it to my office thirty minutes later. I felt bad to have her come meet with this woman. I didn't want her stressing out over anything. The doctor had already told her to take it easy.

"I have never heard of a company making too much money." Viviana tried to hold back her disapproval.

"Well, there was a discrepancy with your pay in taxes."

"Show me, as I am the one who keeps up with her tax documents." Viviana placed her bag in the seat next to her, and waited for Agent Lang to make a move.

"I will be glad to. Do you have her tax forms with you?"

"Yes, do you?" Viviana asked her, and Agent Lang hesitated for a half a second. She took a seat and began going through her bag.

"Well, can you at least tell me what was wrong with her tax documents? Since that's what you're here for."

I was furious. I couldn't sit in the room with this lady anymore. I needed to talk to Jaslynn. She could have informed me that Agent Lang had arrived at my office again.

"Why didn't you text me that she was here?" I whispered to Jaslynn, when I was close enough for only her to hear me.

"You deserve to have peace on your break." She responded nonchalantly. "Secondly, I wanted to watch her. I don't really trust her."

"Did you see anything?"

"No. Her phone didn't even ring one time. I know that doesn't sound like much, but if you're on the clock and you haven't made it back to your headquarters around closing hours, you don't think someone would have called to check on you?"

I understood where Jaslynn was going with this. "So what do you think? She couldn't have spoken to her boss or whoever before she came in."

"Has her phone ever rung? Plus, I've never seen a laptop or a badge. She's a government worker. I know she should at least have a badge." She stopped to think about what she was saying. "I don't know. I could be looking for a reason to trust her, but I don't."

Jaslynn was right. I hadn't seen a badge either.

I headed straight to the back and barged inside of the conference room.

"Let me see your badge, Agent Lang." I commanded.

"Excuse me?" Agent Lang looked offended, and a confused look crossed Viviana's face.

"I need to see your badge. You've been looking through my private business documents, and you've never shown a badge.

"Okay, there is no need to be rude. Here is my badge." She pulled a badge from her messenger bag, and held it up.

I looked at for the IRS logo, and to make sure all of the words were spelled correctly, because I wasn't sure how to authenticate it. "Hmm." I was trying to make her uncomfortable to see how she would react.

"It's clear to me that you aren't comfortable with me being here, so I will have my manger call you within the week, and we'll bring you in for a meeting." She took her badge from me, and grabbed all of her things. "I do apologize for any inconvenience I've caused you. That was never my intention." Her voice was very apologetic, and for a brief moment I felt bad for my behavior.

"Uh-huh." I kept my defensive attitude going. I could tell she was very uncomfortable and I wanted her out of my building.

We walked her to the front door and watched her leave. Me and the girls all stood in the front area and watched her pull off in her car.

"So what do you think, Boss?" Jaslynn was standing up behind her desk.

"I don't trust that bitch." I answered her.

CHAPTER TWENTY

Courtland

"Hey, my dear, what's up?" Melanie said. I hated that I was about to cancel my date with Melanie, but I wasn't in the mood to go out.

"Nothing. I wanted to give you a ring, and let you know that I have to cancel tonight."

"Really?" I could hear the disappointment in her voice.

"I'm so sorry, Baby. I have a situation at work that needs my immediate attention."

"No worries. I understand." Her tone was a bit aggressive, so I knew she wasn't pleased.

"Maybe we can get together tomorrow." I tried to find an alternative. I really enjoyed myself with Melanie, but these days I was so confused with everything that was happening with Sin. I hated to bring Melanie into my mixed emotional situation. I had to get my mind straight.

"No, I have to finish some editing for next month's issue. I plan to be at the office all day." I knew she would say no. She wasn't happy about my last minute cancelation, but I wanted to make sure I made it up to her in a timely matter.

"Well, would you like to go to dinner with me on Thursday?" Today was Sunday, so that would give me a couple of days to get myself together.

"That sounds good." She sounded happier, but I knew she was still disappointed.

"Again, I'm sorry, Baby."

"Don't work too hard, Courtland. I'll see you Thursday." She hung up the phone before I could say goodbye. I leaned back in my chair trying to clear my head. I hope I didn't fuck this up too bad.

I reached for my phone and dialed Sin's number. I needed to talk to her. I hadn't heard from her in the past few days, and I needed to know that she was okay. She didn't pick up.

I called Sin's number four times in a row. *Where in the hell is she?*

Since we last saw each other she had started acting really secretive and I wasn't sure why. She wasn't always answering my phone calls and she hadn't made an effort to return the calls she had missed. I wanted to make sure she wasn't slipping into depression or going back to her old drinking ways. I knew she was hurting, but she seemed to have been doing better this week. I just needed to hear it from her mouth that she was doing fine.

"Man, what are you still doing here?" Damien walked into my office. I tried not to work too late, since most times he or Jenna would be there to help the manager on duty close. "I thought you had a date with Melanie tonight."

"Yeah, I just cancelled." I called Sin's number again.

"What's going on?" Damien looked worried about me. I knew I had ruffled his feathers with the Sin situation so I had been trying to keep as much of my dealings with her to myself.

"Nothing." I hung up my phone since she didn't pick up.

Damien came into my office and closed the door behind him. "What's going on? Did something happen between you and Melanie?"

"No. No. Nothing like that." I knew he really liked Melanie for me, but she wasn't the woman I loved. I cared for her deeply, but it wasn't the same.

"So what's got you so perplexed?"

"I was just checking on Sin. Nothing serious." I was trying to sound casual.

"Holy shit! That is serious." He took a seat. "Is she still hurting over the situation with that guy?"

"I wouldn't say that she's hurting as bad. I think she's gotten over the devastation of the situation. I'm just a little worried about her. I don't want her to spiral out of control. She's back on top, and I want to make sure she stays there." I kept thinking back to when she was drinking. She wasn't herself and she lost a lot of time she couldn't get back. I was thankful that she was able to find her way back from that.

"Wait, what about Melanie? You aren't dropping what you have with her for Sin, are you?"

"You act like what I had with Sin was something bad, and what I have with Melanie is serious."

"So you and Melanie aren't serious now?" He looked at me like he knew I was lying.

Downplaying my relationship with Melanie didn't impress him. Melanie and I had already established that we were taking things slowly, but that wasn't any of his business.

"She's a great girl, but we are only dating. We were never official."

"I wonder if she thinks that." He folded his arms across his chest.

"Okay, well I'm leaving for the day." I rose to my feet. I wasn't in the mood to be scolded. I didn't need to explain my relationships or what I was doing to Damien. Melanie knew we weren't official and that's all that mattered.

"I'm just saying, man, be careful. You were happy with Melanie. You're at the top of your game, and I don't want you to be knocked off by making rash decisions."

"You're right, man. Thanks." I touched his shoulder and walked out of my office. I didn't want to argue with a grown man about my romantic affairs. I would be at the top of my game no matter who I decided to be with, but I appreciated his concern.

I was heading down the hallway when Jenna came around the corner looking happy as usual.

"And where are you off to, Sir?" she asked in a pleasant tone.

"Going out to run some errands. I'll see you tomorrow." I kept walking past her.

"Okay, well someone named Jackson Kensington is on the phone for you. Would you like me to tell him you've left for the evening?"

I stopped in my tracks. "Excuse me?" I turned to her.

"Do you want me to take a message? His name is Jackson Kensington. He says it's urgent and that you already know who he is." She held a phone towards me. I was so busy trying to get past her I didn't even realize she was holding it.

I grabbed the phone and headed back to my office.

"Hello?" I answered in a confused tone. My brother, Jackson, couldn't be on the other line because he was in jail, and I know Jenna didn't accept any charges from a correctional facility.

"Hey, Big Brother." His voice was calm yet firm.

"How did you get this number?" I slammed the office door behind me.

"Now, you know money can buy you anything." He spoke in a laid-back tone, as if he had no cares at all.

"But that's the thing, you don't have any money. You're in jail, Jackson."

"Yeah, you're right." He laughed. "How's life on the outside?"

"What do you want?" I didn't have any time for small talk.

"I'm just calling to see how our company is going. I understand it's doing quite well."

"You've invested no money into my company, so you need not ask any questions about my company matters."

"You sound so tense. Lighten up, Bro. I know you need me, just know I got you when I get out. I don't have long in here, and I've already spoken to my attorneys and they've written up a contract I think you will be more than happy to sign. I can't wait to be your partner, Big Brother."

"Trust me when I say, I don't need you. You were never on my team and you never will be. Do not call my phone again." I hung up the phone. I wasn't sure what kind of sick, twisted game Jackson was trying to play, but I didn't have time to participate. I should have gotten all of the information from him, but I refused to accept any money from him. He would not be a partner in my company.

I sat back down in my chair. I said a quick prayer, because I was on the top of my game, and I wasn't sure what could possibly happen next. I refused to let my company be dragged like the Kensington name was. I had to let my past go, because it was only a hindrance to my future, and I didn't need anyone from my past trying to make themselves relevant in my life again.

I reached for my cell phone that was ringing in my pocket. Sin was finally calling me back, but I didn't pick up. Maybe Damien was right. Maybe I didn't need to entertain the past, and Sin was the past.

I grabbed my keys, and headed to surprise Melanie with a visit. She didn't deserve to be cancelled on last minute, and I didn't want to be alone.

I jumped on the interstate and headed to her quaint suburb outside of Atlanta. It didn't take me long to get to Melanie's house. I got out of my truck, went to the door, and rang the doorbell. All of the lights were out in the front of the house. *Hmmm, she should be home.* I rang the doorbell again, because I was surprised that she hadn't come to the door.

I dialed her number, trying to reach her, but she didn't pick up. I went back to my truck to wait for a couple of minutes. I figured that I did pop up unannounced so I was okay with giving her a moment to get back with me. After ten minutes of waiting, I texted her letting her know that I stopped by to see her. She didn't promptly respond, so I backed out of her driveway, and headed back to Atlanta.

My phone sounded, letting me know I had received a text message. I pulled over to the side of the road to check and see if Melanie was finally responding to me. It was Sin.

174

"Hey! I'm just getting home. Sorry, had a meeting. Let me know if you need me," the message read. I pulled back into the street and headed to Sin's house. I had some time on my hands, and nothing to do. She had some explaining to do herself because I didn't understand why she had become so secretive all of a sudden.

CHAPTER TWENTY-ONE

Sinaiyah

Courtland was sitting next to me at my bar eating hot wings and fries that we ordered from the wing spot down the street from my building. I never knew him to be a wing guy, but he was in the mood for wings, so that's what I ordered.

"Thanks, Babe." He was licking sauce off his fingers.

"Anytime." It felt good to have him in my intimate space again and hear him calling me babe. I wasn't expecting him to spend the night, but we had a lot to catch up on apparently.

"So what is on your schedule today?" He turned towards me, and took a big gulp of lemonade.

"I'm going to meet with Heather-Nicole a little later. What about you?" He gave me a confused side-eye. "Yeah. She wants to talk."

"Let's go ice-skating." He changed the subject.

I couldn't believe what I was hearing. I couldn't even imagine Courtland on skates. I missed his spontaneity, but I wasn't in the mood to ice-skate.

"Are there any ice-skating rinks in the city?" It was fall, but I wasn't sure if it was ice-skating season just yet.

"Put some jeans on and let's go." He wasn't asking me; he was telling me.

I decided to go with the flow, because he was in a mood last night when he came over. He was acting like I owed him an explanation as to why I had been distant. Truth was, I wasn't trying to distance myself from him. I actually wanted him around more, but I was trying to keep myself protected. Landon was still around and I needed to keep a straight face with him and a clear mind, as well as figure out how I wanted to expose his infidelity. I was torn because I didn't want to cause any more harm to Heather-Nicole. Seeing her break down last week with Viviana broke my heart.

"Okay. I'm ready." I walked out of my bathroom fifteen minutes later dressed in a pair of dark jeans and a denim button down shirt. I decided to pull my hair up, and I had filled in my brows, added mascara, and put on a dark shade of purple on my lips.

"My, my, my, you look gorgeous." He was dressed in his Marc Jacobs burgundy collar sweater and a pair of dark jeans.

"So do you. Where did this sweater come from?" I couldn't help myself from asking, since it wasn't what he had on yesterday when he came over.

"You must have forgotten." He laughed. "I keep a few items in this drawer." He pointed to my bottom dresser drawer.

I thought to myself for a moment to try and remember. It had been so long since he was in my bedroom, and even longer since he had changed clothes in my condo. "I must have." I was still a little confused.

"Yeah. I forgot all about this sweater." He gave himself another glance over in the mirror. "We need socks," he shouted.

"I got it." I went to my dresser and pulled out a two thick pairs of black socks.

"Grab two more pairs, please."

"Do we need four pairs of socks, Courtland?" I felt like he was being extra, but I grabbed another two pairs anyway.

"Alright. Let's go!" He was so excited.

I still wasn't in the mood to skate, but I had already decided to be a good sport. What I couldn't wait for was to see him fall.

The rink was fairly empty when we got inside, but it was nice. I hadn't been ice-skating since I was in college, with my girlfriends.

"Thanks, Baby." Courtland laced up my skates for me. I took the frown off my face and grabbed his hand. "Now, let's get one thing straight. I'm not holding your hand while we skate. I don't know how good you are, and I don't want to be falling everywhere." My biggest fear was falling on the ice, someone skating on my hand,

and cutting me. The rink wasn't packed, but I still didn't want any crazy injuries.

"Have it your way then." He let go of me and jumped on ice.

I had to hold onto the rail as I wobbled to get on the ice and I almost fell. Courtland was halfway around the rink by the time I got both feet inside the rink. *Show off.* Who knew he could skate?

"Excuse me, ma'am, it looks like you need a little help. Are you okay?" I turned around to Courtland skating towards me. He was teasing me, because I hadn't gotten anywhere and he was starting his second lap.

"Oh shut-up, Courtland!" We both laughed.

"You ready to hold my hand now?" He reached his hand out towards mine and I grabbed it.

We skated for a good hour and I couldn't do anymore. I forgot how torturous skating was for my entire body.

"You treat me so good," I said as Courtland was unlacing my skates. When he pulled off my skates, my socks were soaking wet.

"Now you see why we needed the extra pairs of socks.

"Yeah." I laughed. He had won that one, because I was trying to be a hard ass with him earlier.

After he took off his skates and turned both of our skates in, we headed back to the car. I struggled trying to get into his truck. My thighs were hurting something serious and the balls of my feet were sore.

"Did you enjoy yourself despite the pain?" He couldn't tell if I was happy with our random outing or not.

"I did. You know I enjoy your spontaneous side."

"Good." He rubbed my hand, and we headed back to my house.

I was too tired to meet with Heather-Nicole, but I decided to go ahead and meet her. Since I had already eaten, I decided to meet her at a cupcake shop down the street from my building, that way I didn't have to go too far and it was in walking distance from my house.

"How are you feeling?" We took a seat at a table near the window. She looked terrible. Her skin was pale, her hair looked like she hadn't brushed it in days, and she was wearing sweats. She didn't look like the eccentric lady that I met last week.

"I'm trying to keep myself together. I don't know how long I can continue acting like I don't know that he's spending the extra time he does have with you."

"Now, I'm not telling you this to hurt you, but I've only seen him once since I last saw you. We're also going to a poetry event tomorrow. If it makes you feel better, I'm not enjoying myself." She laughed. It was hard for me to spend time with him knowing he has a wife, but what I had in mind needed a little more time, and lots of planning.

"Thanks for letting me know." I could tell it wasn't sitting well with her.

"Isn't his birthday coming up soon?"

"Yeah, in a couple of days, actually. Why?"

"I want to make it an eventful one. That's the only reason why I haven't said anything yet."

"What are you thinking?" She was hesitant. "I just don't want this to backfire on me. He won't let me divorce him, and he said if I tried he would take the kids from me, and I'll be left with absolutely nothing. He told me that when I found out about the last chick he cheated with."

I couldn't believe what she was saying. When we were younger, I never knew Landon to be so cruel. He was a true manipulator, and listening to Heather-Nicole, was helping me to see that this is who is really is.

"I can't believe he threatened to take your kids and your life away from you."

"I should have known when he swept me off my feet that this would happen, but I was so in love with him." Heather-Nicole finished her story. "He made me feel so special, but he's made it completely clear that I am replaceable." She quickly wiped a tear from her eye.

"No, please don't cry." I handed her a napkin. "You've really opened my eyes to him. To know him as a man is quite different from the young man I used to be in love with."

"I didn't know he had unfinished business with you." She dabbed at her eye to even out her puffy eyes.

"The only unfinished business I have with him is making him wish he had never come back into my life."

"I don't' want you to go out of your way for me. I just want to get out of this marriage, and move on with my life."

"When I'm done, you'll be holding his balls and will be calling all the shots. Trust me." I tried to assure her, but she was distraught. "Trust me, there is always a loop hole."

"He's a lawyer, and he has lots of lawyer friends that he claims owe him favors. I know I can't win against him." She looked helpless, slumped over in her seat.

"I know lawyers, too. I can put you in touch with some great people."

"Yeah, but I'm sure I won't be able to afford it. You don't have to do anything for me, I will figure this out." She rose from her seat and headed out the front door. I watched her go down the street from the window as I finished my cupcake. I went back and got another cupcake, because this situation had stressed me out.

I called Courtland, but he didn't answer. I could really use his shoulder to lean on.

I left the cupcake shop and headed back to my building. I took my time walking back. Hearing everything Heather-Nicole said really upset me. My emotions were all over the place. I felt bad for Heather-Nicole. She didn't deserve to be treated so terribly. Every fiber in me wanted to call Landon and tell him off. He had been trying to live a double lifestyle for far too long.

My phone started ringing, and I was in no rush to answer it. I figured it was Courtland calling me back. I fished for my phone in my purse to confirm my guess, but it was Viviana.

"Yes, ma'am?" I answered quickly before she was sent to my voicemail.

"How did your meeting go?"

"Heather-Nicole doesn't look good," I shook my head.

"Oh goodness," she sighed into the phone.

"She doesn't deserve this. I want to believe that she's lying and over exaggerating this, but she doesn't have any reason to lie, and even if she was, I still wouldn't want anything to do with Landon because he is married with a family."

"I get it, Sin. You know I get it." Her voice was calm.

"He's going to know that he fucked over the wrong woman, and I hope that she can find the strength to fight him in court."

"She has two kids she'll win. She may not have the man, but she will have his money. Trust me."

"Oh, I didn't tell you: she said that she tried to divorce him the last time he cheated, but he threatened to take the kids and everything she loved away from her."

"He said what?" she screamed in my ear.

"Yes, ma'am. I'm ashamed I ever fell in love with him. He's a pitiful man."

"Lord, help. That's why she broke down in my office. She's reliving the same nightmare. She was probably just getting her head above water, and then here you come."

"Right, and I feel bad. I would have never given him a chance to prove himself to me, and I for damn sure would have never given his ass some. I'm so fucking pissed off about this shit I don't know what to do." I was heated.

"I know, Sin, but keep calm, honey. When will you see him again?"

"We are going to a poetry reading later this week."

"Oh, that's different."

"Yeah, I know." I chuckled. "If only I was going with a man that was worth a damn."

"Well, you do have a point. Just stay calm. I know you have a plan, but keep me posted on how you want handle this. I don't want you caught up in no mess."

"Oh, you'll know every step I take with him. I may need Damien's assistance, too."

"Well, you know he's down to help any way he can."

"Yeah. I need to talk to him. I just don't want Courtland in any of this, and I know they run together."

"Yeah, you're right."

"Well, put your feet up and get some rest. You need anything?"

"Nope. We good over here, but thank you."

"Of course, my dear. I'll hit you back later."

"Okay! Cool."

I hung up the phone and walked into my building. I was ready to get in my bed with a glass of wine.

CHAPTER TWENTY-TWO

Courtland

I felt refreshed when I woke up. Spending yesterday with Sin was good for me. Everything felt perfect. The day was perfect, our date was perfect, and she was perfect.

I got up from my bed to get my day started. I had laid down long enough. I went to the kitchen to find something to eat.

There was barely food in the refrigerator. I was never home enough to really stock up on food, but I did have my necessities. I decided to whip up a protein shake and eat some blueberries. That was the only real option I had, because I wasn't in the mood to cook anything serious.

I walked back to my room with my blueberries and shake and got back in the bed. It felt good to just relax with no worries. This was the life I really enjoyed. My condo was peaceful. The sun was shining bright, lighting up my room, and it was quiet.

My phone was buzzing like crazy, but I wanted to enjoy my shake in peace, so I didn't answer it.

After I finished my shake, I washed the glass out and threw away the empty blueberry container. I headed back to my room to finally check my messages. It wasn't anything important, so I was happy I let myself enjoy my moment of peace. My phone started buzzing again in my hand.

"Hey, Jenna."

"Hey. I wanted to let you know that Mr. Kensington had his lawyers drop some papers off at the office this morning. Also, he called here again today to say he wasn't able to get you on your cell."

"Papers?" I was trying to hold in my anger until I had all the facts.

"He wants to be an investor," she started singing in my ear. "He says that you all have spoken about this, and he wanted to send over an agreement that he would like for you to go over and sign. Isn't this exciting?"

I was heated. "What the fuck, Jenna? Hell no. This shit isn't exciting. It's a fucking tragedy. We will not be doing any business with him. Tear that shit up!"

"Oh, wow. Well, umm." She was hesitant to say whatever was on her mind. "I, umm, I sent over our investment packet to him."

"What's all in the packet?" I couldn't remember. I remembered going through some of the packet, but not everything. I said a silent prayer that this didn't get any worse.

"Well, it does have a few of our earnings, and some of our projected earnings for the upcoming year,

187

nothing detailed. It's almost like a welcome packet. Don't you remember approving it?" She paused waiting for me to respond, but I remained quiet. "Okay. I invited him in, and he said he wanted to meet with you as well. He said he was interested in the growth of our company, and that he was expecting our packet. I figured I had missed something, so I sent it."

"Sent it where?" I was confused. She couldn't have sent it to the county jail.

"With his lawyer."

"No, Jenna! You hadn't missed a thing. He is a major threat to our company. He manipulated you. Always contact me when it comes to a potential investor. I can't believe you could act so irresponsibly." I didn't mean to lash out at Jenna, but I was frustrated. There was no telling what he could do with such personal information about my company.

"I didn't know." Her voice was quiet.

"How could you know? You never asked! Did you do any research on him? Do you know the name of his company? Does he even have a company? You do your research first!" I was sitting straight up in my bed.

"Whoa. Whoa. Whoa." She was speaking very calmly. "You haven't told me anything about Mr. Kensington. I treated him like I would treat any potential investor, with respect. He asked for more information, and I gave it to him, just as I would with any other potential investor. Whatever problems you had with him in the past are between you and him, because you never made me aware that he would be a threat to the company."

"Damn, Jenna!" I hated that she had a point. "I'm on my way. We'll talk when I get there." I hung up and punched the wall. I didn't care that I left a dent in my living room wall.

Jackson was trying to ruin my company from jail, and that shit was not about to happen. My day was going so fucking great before this shit.

I hurried to get dressed. I needed to get to the office quickly.

I walked towards my car in the garage. "Man, are you busy?" I thought I had handled this situation with Jackson, but clearly he didn't respect my peaceful approach. Now I had to get Damien involved.

"I'm leaving the doctor's office. I'll be back at the office in thirty minutes. Is everything okay?" He sounded like he was stressed out.

"We'll talk when you get there. I'm heading there now. Are you okay?"

"Yeah, man. I'll head straight to your office when I get there. Cool?"

"Yeah." I hung up the phone and sped to the Palace. I flew through the Atlanta streets trying to hurry and get to my office. I needed to get to Jenna and figure this mess out.

Jackson had called the office before, but now he's prying for information, and he succeeded for the most part. I didn't appreciate him taking advantage of my assistant. Jenna was about business, and I guess he picked up on that. She invited him to come in if he wanted to discuss becoming a partner, and I wondered how he planned on coming in.

I pulled into my assigned parking spot and headed inside. The Palace was crowded. I took a deep breath when I walked inside. I reminded myself that I couldn't be upset with Jenna. She didn't know I had a brother who was trying to push his way back into my life.

I didn't see Jenna on the main level. I headed to my office upstairs. It was quiet; no one was on the floor. I was trying to get all of my thoughts together. I didn't understand what Jackson's logic was. And I could have sworn that he would be in jail for at least eight years; he shouldn't be getting out any time soon. I was pacing my office floor.

Jenna walked in my office with Damien on her heels. She looked so nervous standing behind him. I was certain that she had tried to catch Damien up on what had happened, and from her nervous look, I could only guess that he told her who Mr. Kensington really was.

I walked behind my desk.

"So Jackson has been calling up here, and you're just now saying something?" Damien's voice was filled with anger as he walked all the way up to my desk. I rested both hands on my desk so that we could be face-to-face. "How long has this been going on?"

"Ask Jenna. She's the one who's been talking to him and sending him information without discussing it with me."

She was standing quietly near the door. "It started with him calling a few times, but now he's been calling every day," she explained. "He seems to know a lot about the company already. He's clearly been doing his research." She spoke up loud enough to be heard.

"Things like what?" Damien turned around and looked at her.

"Like how many members we have, how much money we've been bringing in on a monthly basis, who the members of our staff are, who we're contracting services from, and things of that nature." She spoke clearly.

"How the fuck does he know this?" Damien turned back around with his hands in the air.

"I don't know, but I refuse for Jackson to terrorize me and my company from a fucking jail cell!"

"Wait, he's doing all of this from jail?" Jenna was confused. "Isn't that illegal?"

"Yeah. I'm going to look into this." Damien was heading for the door.

"Please do, because if Jackson is prying that means Victoria isn't too far behind him." I didn't want to say it, but it was the truth. Jackson was her favorite son, and he would do anything she told him to do.

"Shit, man! Things were finally settling down. We can't let her come back and ruin our company." Damien looked like he was ready to attack me.

"She won't. I have every intention to beat them at their own game." I turned to Jenna. "We need to seal our documents and go through our members. There has to be a snake in the grass, and we need to find it and cut its head off."

"Yes, sir." She dismissed herself and closed the door behind her.

"Man, what the fuck is going on?" Damien walked back over to where I was standing

"I should have known it was coming. You know they weren't going to let me be on top for long. Victoria despises me, and Jackson does too." I took a seat at my desk. I was starting to get a headache from the stress.

"Victoria is going to slip up, and I'm going to find her." Damien was pacing, with his arms folded across his chest.

"Yeah, but she's already found us." I felt defeated.

Damien sat down in a chair across from my desk. He leaned his head in his hands. "What does she want? She has money, and she disappeared so quickly, I thought she had moved on with her life."

"She wants to see me fail, that's all. Victoria has been gone so long, I started to think she was dead, and I was okay with that."

"I think we all would be okay with that." Damien added.

"No hard feelings, I get it." I had prayed that she was dead. Nobody missed her presence; life was so much better with her not being around. "I'm worried about Sin. If Victoria is out to get me, I know she's got her nose in Sin's business, too. Remember, Sin walked away without getting any heat from the courts." I prayed silently that Victoria wasn't behind this. Victoria and Jackson got everything they deserved.

Damien looked at me with a blank stare. "Uh-uh, man, my woman is connected to Sin. I can't have my woman in no mess." The blankness in his eyes filled with rage.

"We're going to figure this out."

"I'm serious. We're doing too well to have Victoria be our demise."

He was right. I couldn't let her destroy everything I had built because she wasn't happy with herself. "She is trying to be the death of me." I leaned back in my seat. I was irritated. My day had started off so perfectly, and now it had gone to hell.

"And that can't happen." He leaned back in his seat. Something was on his mind.

"It won't. What's going on with you?"

He took a deep breath and looked at me. "Look, I'm planning to propose to Viv soon."

"Wait, what?" I was thrown off by his talk about proposing. He hadn't told me that he had thought about proposing. I knew they were serious but I didn't know he was ready to really commit.

"Yeah."

"When are you going to ask her?"

"We've already talked about marriage. She has a ring already, but I still plan to officially ask."

"Wow." I couldn't believe that they had kept this from me.

"Sorry, man, we just decided to keep it private for a while. We were going to let you know, but a lot has been happening."

"I understand."

"Yeah, and I want to let you know that we're expecting our first child."

I was blown away by this news. "Viv is pregnant?"

"Yeah, we were keeping it a secret until after her first trimester. She was having a little difficulty, but everything is good. She and the baby are fine now."

Now I understood why he was so mad. He had to provide for his family and didn't have time to be caught up in any scandals. I still couldn't believe that my best friend was pregnant and hadn't told me. Now I really regretted bringing her into my mess with Landon. Damien had every reason to be angry with me that evening.

It was my duty to make sure that nothing happened to my company, because if something happened it would have a negative ripple effect.

CHAPTER TWENTY-THREE

Sinaiyah

It was Landon's idea to come to this little hole in the wall jazz spot. It was cute inside. The lights were dimmed and full of smoke from the hookahs. We were able to get a sweet corner spot in the back. I was disgusted to be sitting so close to him this evening. I couldn't look at him the same way after everything Heather-Nicole had told me. I had a whole new level of disgust with him. I had tried to cancel on him tonight, but he was persistent.

The artists were so raw. I really enjoyed listening to them. Some of the topics were extremely deep. I felt like I was watching a chopped up soap opera. They spoke on rape, molestation, drunkenness, and so much more; no topic was left uncovered.

"How you feeling?" Landon was rubbing my inner thigh and my skin crawled in the worst way.

"Good. You?" I felt really uncomfortable sitting beside him. I hadn't seen him in about a week, because I was playing the 'I'm busy' card real hard.

"I'm awesome."

"That's good. Somebody's birthday is coming up." I winked at Landon. One thing I had learned from this situation was that it is hard to pretend when you don't care anymore.

"You know what, you're right!" He played along with me.

"I want to plan something amazing. My surprises are always a lot of fun."

"I want the surprise!" He raised his hand like a child in class.

"You are so silly." I tried to laugh away my disgust, because I could feel a frown beginning to form.

"So what you got planned? You know you don't have to do anything, right?"

It was almost cute that he didn't want me to feel any pressure. I didn't want to do anything for him, but I did need to make him feel special, despite the scum he truly was.

"Since you're mine, I want to show you how special you are to me."

"But I already know." He leaned in and kissed my lips. I gave him a quick peck. I didn't want him lingering on my lips longer than he had to.

"Oh, really? So you don't want my gift?"

"Of course I do." His eyes were bright.

"You don't know how excited I am right now." And he didn't know, but he was going to find out really soon. I had an idea of what I wanted to do, and I knew it was going to be eventful.

We stopped talking so that we could hear the next poet perform. I really loved hearing the different artists give their testimonies. I also enjoyed the fact that my conversation with Landon was limited due to the many performers. I didn't have much to say to him these days anyway.

The spot was really calm, and I couldn't stop looking at the art covering the walls. It was nice to see all of the couples and groups of friends sitting together in a trance by each artist.

When the last artist finished, the room got loud with laughter and conversation. Music started playing and some people started dancing. It felt good to be out in a different crowd. There was no specific age group tonight, just people who enjoyed the arts. I was happy to be in this number, because I loved the arts.

"So have you missed me?" Landon broke my thoughts.

"I sure have, so where have you been?" I tried to fix the scowl on my face. Why would he ask me such a dumb question?

"Working."

"Oh, really? I was starting to think that you had a secret life, with a wife and kids, that you needed to get back to."

He laughed really hard. "Oh, no, I don't have those types of responsibilities." He brushed off my comment.

I nodded my head in amusement. He blatantly lied to me with a straight face. I wasn't expecting the truth from him, but he didn't hesitate with his lie, and that amused me. "I know you're busy, so I don't hold it against you." I smiled at him. "I can't get mad at having a working man in my life."

He winked at me. "I love that you are so understanding. That's why you're going to be my woman real soon." He gave me a kiss on the cheek. "I wasn't sure at first with the way you were kicking me to the curb. But the real question is where have you been? You've been so busy lately."

I laughed to keep from crying. Now I wished I had kicked his ass beyond the curb and into another country. "You came out of nowhere. I wasn't sure if I could trust you. I do apologize for being so busy. You know my company is still new and I handle a lot of the day to day duties on my own."

"I know. I'm still very proud of you." He kissed my cheek. "So how do you feel now? Haven't I proven to you that I'm not here to hurt you?"

My body tensed up and my skin crawled. I wanted to tell him that he was the scum of the earth and that he wasn't worth shit, but I didn't. "Yes, Landon, you have proven yourself well." I continued with my task of making him feel special.

"Thank you. You're so kind." He joked.

"Well, I'm getting tired. I told you about that big meeting I have in the morning. I still need to go over some documents and get some rest. Do you mind if we call it an early night?"

"I really hate to, but we can if you insist."

"I'm sorry, but I have something amazing planned for your birthday that will more than make up for ending our night early." I tried to look at him with tired eyes.

"Well, I'll let you go tonight, but only because I'll see you Sunday. That's not too long of a wait."

We walked to the car, and headed back to my place. It felt good outside and the streets weren't crowded at all. He dropped me off at my condo about ten minutes later. That's what I loved about living in Atlanta. It didn't take me long to get home. I lived in the heart of the city and everything was close by. I was a true city girl.

I poured myself a glass of wine and headed to my bedroom to watch a little television. Although the poetry reading was great, living a lie was draining. Landon had to have started believing his own lie, because he really didn't see himself as a married man, and that scared me. I didn't understand why someone would marry another individual if they didn't really want him or her in their future. What did Heather-Nicole have that Landon had to marry her? Maybe she had money, or maybe she bankrolled his company. It really didn't matter what the reason was, all that mattered was that he was married to her, and he wasn't trying to let her go, or at least that's how I felt from what she had told me. For all I know, she could have been a gold-digger that trapped him, and he found out too late. It was confusing because he married this woman, had kids with her, came looking for me, and then insinuated that we would get married. Maybe he believed in polygamy.

I was embarrassed that I allowed him into my life, my house, and me. He didn't deserve anything I had to offer.

I got comfortable under my covers and tried to get some sleep. I couldn't stop tossing and turning, because I was so frustrated. I couldn't stop thinking about Landon and how stupid I was.

I finally went to sleep at four-twenty in the morning, and I was back up staring at the clock at eight-fifty.

I wasn't going into the office until noon. I had made plans to meet with Heather-Nicole to eat breakfast at ten.

I got out of bed to get my day started. I already couldn't wait for this day to be over.

I decided to wear my hair down in curls, and I did my ten-minute face. Every time I went into the office, I liked to look as natural as possible. Since I was in the beauty business, my clients looked to me as the actual doctor beauty, and I always wanted them to see how healthy my skin was. I made it out of the house by a quarter to ten.

Heather-Nicole was already seated at a table when I made it to the Flying Biscuit. I was in the mood for some biscuits and grits.

"Good morning." She stood up and gave me a hug. It was awkward to have a relationship with her. She was married to a man that I used to be in love with. It was straight up weird to me, but I went along with it.

"Hello, dear, you look good." I wasn't lying. She looked happier, her skin was glowing, and she was wearing some badass, plum, thigh high boots that matched her hat perfectly. Heather-Nicole was fierce. "Where are you going after this?"

"Girl, nowhere. Maybe to the mall, but nowhere special."

"Well, don't go overboard buying stuff you don't need." I teased.

She laughed out loud. "Girl, you so silly. I have to get dressed, and get out the house, to feel good about myself."

"Oh no," I felt sorry for her.

The waitress came to the table and took our orders. It had been a long time since I had been here, but my order always remained the same: shrimp and grits with a sweet tea on the side.

"So you're not working?"

"Girl, no. Landon doesn't want me working." She rolled her eyes towards the ceiling. "I was working in marketing, but he wanted me at home. But I can't say that it was all him. I wanted to raise our kids."

"That's nice. How are your babies?" It was weird to ask about her kids, but it couldn't hurt.

"Fine. Spoiled rotten. Nothing new." She took a sip from her sweet tea.

"So what did you want to talk about?"

"I just wanted to know what your next move was." She leaned in towards me.

I hadn't told anyone what I was planning for Landon's birthday, because I wasn't sure what I wanted to do. "What do you think I should do?" I was curious if she had thought of anything.

"That's all you. I just want to know if I can be a part of your plan. You said that you had something planned for him. I want him to know that he can't hide from me. Also, I'm interested in what's going to happen so that I can know how to plan to protect my children. I need to know what's up your sleeve, because what you decide will affect me and my household in some way.

"I understand, and I don't want to put you in a hurtful situation. Did you want to be there when I confront him?"

"Listen, listen." She laughed and held her hands up in the air. "I may not know what you are thinking about doing, but I know I don't want any part in it. I've accepted my role in his life. I don't mean nothing to that man, and that's okay. I'm just going to do what I need to do to survive."

The waitress brought us our food. I was thankful for the brief intermission.

"But you don't live this life to just survive, Heather-Nicole. You live this life to love, to grow, and to learn." I felt pity for this woman.

"Fuck all of that, I'm happy."

I looked over her hard. "No, you are not, but you do whatever the hell you want to do." I didn't have time to argue.

"I am happy, and I have been doing what I want." She was eating a breakfast bowl.

"And how's that been going for you?" I was asking her seriously.

"Terrific!"

"Okay. As long as you're happy."

"Don't act like you really give a damn about my happiness."

"What would make you say that?" I was surprised to hear her say that.

"If you cared about my happiness, you wouldn't be still sleeping with my husband."

"I see." I took another bite of my food.

"But we aren't friends, you're just the mistress." She looked at me with hate filled eyes.

"To be completely honest, I haven't slept with your husband since I found out about you last week." I was trying to keep my voice steady. I didn't want this to turn ugly.

"So is that supposed to make me respect you?"

"Okay." I put my fork down. I was happy that I was able to eat the majority of my food. "You're the one whose worth has diminished in the eyes of her husband. I was trying to help you and your situation."

"My situation doesn't need help, and I know I may not mean much to my husband, but he doesn't want me to go." She smirked as though she was winning.

"Yeah." I was done with this situation. Maybe she was dumb. "Jesus didn't die on the cross for me to show you your worth. If you want to settle for less than what you deserve, go right ahead."

"You know what, you have a lot of nerve coming here like you're doing me a favor. I didn't ask you for a damn thang. I don't need to get revenge to find happiness. I'm happy with myself. I will figure this out, and if I need your assistance, I'll call you, but until then, you can go."

I couldn't believe that she was talking to me like this. I was happy to hear how she really felt about me, and not watching her pretend as if we were friends. I hadn't realized I was trying to get revenge so that I could be happy with myself. Landon had hurt me to my core, and I hated him for that. I didn't deserve that hurt. I didn't deserve to be mistreated by a man I once loved so dearly.

"You are right, Heather-Nicole. I need revenge. Call me vindictive, call me malicious, hell, you can call me spiteful, but what your husband did to me is unforgivable. I didn't ask him to be a part of my life. He wanted to be a part of my life. He made the decision to be in my life, just like he made the decision to hurt you, continuously. If you're okay with being his doormat, and being his yes doll, then you continue playing your role, but if you haven't figured it out, your husband is shopping for a new woman, and I know he's got you too scared to divorce him. Know he has something planned and his plan doesn't involve you. Don't say I didn't warn you, and don't act devastated when it happens." I stood up from my seat and walked towards the door. She could pay for the tab. I headed down the block to my car. I needed to get to the office anyway. I had four clients for the day.

I sat in my car and let my seat back. I needed a moment to catch my breath. I turned on my car and locked my doors. I couldn't pull away because my hands shaking so badly. Heather-Nicole had struck a nerve. I rested my head on the headrest and closed my eyes.

Vindictive. Malicious. Spiteful. Those weren't words that I ever wanted to be associated with, but I fit the meanings perfectly at this moment. I never thought I would be filled with such hatred for Landon, but I was, and I needed to regain control of myself quickly.

I could hear my phone ringing in my purse, but I wasn't in the mood to answer it. I looked at the clock; it was eleven o'clock. I had been sitting for almost fifteen minutes.

My phone started ringing again. This time I looked down to see who it was. Heather-Nicole's name appeared on my phone. I declined it. I pulled out of my parking spot and pulled into the street. She had called me back to back, but I needed a moment to myself.

My phone started ringing again. Heather-Nicole wouldn't stop calling me.

"Yes," I answered it quickly with the intention of getting off the phone even quicker.

"Where did you go?" She was gasping for air. "We aren't finished talking."

I hung up the phone. I didn't have time to play any more games with her.

CHAPTER TWENTY-FOUR
Courtland

"Shouldn't you be leaving?" Damien was sitting down in my office.

My lawyers had just left with all of the documents that were sent over by Jackson. Damien stayed behind to finish discussing a plan to keep Jackson behind bars. I wasn't as mad anymore. I was trying to stay in a positive place.

"Naw. She's going to meet me at the restaurant."

"Oh okay. How's everything going between you two?"

"Fine. How's Viv?"

"She's fantastic."

"Have you figured out when you're going to propose officially?" I still was in shock that he hadn't told me that they were practically engaged already.

"That's the thing. I haven't figured it all the way out. We've been discussing marriage for a while now. She's the one, man." He looked up at the ceiling. "I just want to make sure I do it right. I've talked to her mom and dad, and they gave me hell, but I have their blessing."

"That's a great thing." They were a lot more serious than I had given them credit for. I didn't know that he had met her family, but I should have known. "When you know, you know." I fully supported this union, and I didn't want him to think I thought otherwise.

"Absolutely." He agreed. "I'm waiting for you to settle down with your right one."

"I was close, but life decided differently." Now all that pressure he was giving me about Melanie made sense.

"So what is going on with you and Sin?"

"We're going to be alright."

"What?" He laughed. "So are you and Sin back on track?"

"We're working on it."

"So, how does Melanie fit into this equation?"

"Man, I don't know." I hadn't really thought about what was going to happen between me and Melanie. I knew that we were going to dinner tonight, and I was going to see how tonight panned out before I made any rash decisions. I didn't want to hurt Melanie, but we had set boundaries in the beginning for our relationship, so I knew I wasn't in too deep.

"Well, don't be late tonight." He stood up and went back to his office.

We had dinner reservations for seven at Maggiano's, since she was in the mood for Italian food. I had a little time on my hands, so I locked up my office and headed to the bar. It was nice to see members enjoying the amenities we offered. The bar was packed. I should have known the bar would be full, because it was happy hour.

I found Jenna and told her I was leaving for the evening. She was still upset with me for withholding information from her, but she kept it professional with me. I realize that I've put her through a lot already. I was definitely going to have to get her a really nice Christmas present.

I decided to go straight to the restaurant and wait for Melanie so that I wouldn't be late. After my surprise visit, she didn't get in contact with me until two days later. I knew she was mad, so I already knew tonight was going to have to be damn near perfect if I wanted her to stick around.

I was seated in a booth in the center of the restaurant. It was crowded, too. I went ahead and ordered a bottle of wine for us and a glass of water for myself.

Melanie arrived right on time. I could tell she was surprised to see me waiting. She was pretty in her grey sweater dress and matching boots.

"Hello, sir." She said, walking towards me. I slid from the table, and got up to greet her properly. I gave her a hug and a kiss. She didn't seem to be in a bad mood, which gave me some relief.

"How are you?" I watched her get comfortable in the booth before I took my seat.

"I'm good. How are you?"

I took my seat. "Brilliant." I was lying, but she didn't need to know about the trouble that was brewing in my company.

"Wow. That's a strong word. Did I miss anything?"

"Nope. I'm just happy I can finally see you."

"Oh, yeah. I'm sorry you drove all the way out to see me and I wasn't there. After you cancelled, my girlfriends came and took me bowling and what not." She waved me off with her hand. I guess this was her explanation, and I had to accept it.

"Understood. Did you enjoy yourself?"

"Ehh. It was a regular night out." She was looking at her menu and she didn't take her eyes off of it.

I felt like she was lying. Melanie was the type of person who always made eye contact. If you weren't strong enough, it would make you uncomfortable.

The waitress came to the table and took our orders. Melanie didn't hesitate looking at the young waitress in the eyes, so I knew something was up. After the waitress left, I sat staring at her. She looked everywhere but my direction.

"Something's on your mind. You care to tell me what it is?" She wasn't going to bring up whatever she was hiding, and I needed to get whatever it was out of the way.

"Huh? What makes you say that?" She still didn't look at me. This time she looked at her wine glass and picked it up to take a sip.

"What is it that you don't want to tell me?"

Her shoulders sunk and a sad expression came over her face. "I think we should take some time apart."

She finally made eye contact with me. I knew for sure that was what was bothering her.

"Wait. Where is this coming from?" I was happy to have her company this evening, and she was breaking things off with me. There had to be more to this story. I knew she wasn't breaking things off because I cancelled one date; there was more to the story.

"Your actions." She answered simply.

Her answer stung me. "What do you mean my actions?" I felt like I had been nothing but a gentleman during our brief dating period.

"I don't have your attention anymore. You're clearly putting your time and energy into something or someone else. And before I start to overthink and make assumptions, I think I need some space."

"You already are overthinking. I am spending my time at the Courtland Palace. I have a lot going on. No one specific person is getting my time or energy, just my company."

"I haven't seen you, Courtland. You forgot about me, or rather, you put me on pause."

"Just because I haven't seen you doesn't mean you haven't crossed my mind." It had been a while since

I had last seen her, but it hadn't been that long. Plus, I was with her now. That had to count for something.

"But that's just it, I've only crossed your mind. You haven't thought of me enough to call or text. I've only been a thought."

"I made time to see you today." With all the shit I had going on at the office, I could have stayed there to handle some more business." I clasped my hands together and looked at her intensely.

"This is just a moment. Honestly, it feels like a sympathy meeting. You don't want me."

"Who do I want then?" I felt like she was hinting about Sin, and I wanted to see if she would actually say that another woman had my attention. I wasn't sure what my response back would be, but she seemed to have all of the answers right now.

"Only you know who you want. I just know, at this moment, I'm not what your heart desires. I am okay with that, are you?"

I leaned back in the booth. Our waitress came with our entrees, and I was no longer in an eating mood anymore. I was hungry, but I would much rather eat with better company. I gave the waitress my card, and told her to go ahead and pay my tab and to pack my food up to-go.

Melanie looked alarmed by my abrupt behavior. I didn't want her to feel like she was eating a sympathy meal. I shouldn't have paid for her meal, but I was a gentleman.

"Really, Courtland?"

I didn't have anything to say to her.

"You're that upset?"

I waited patiently for our waitress to come back. When she did, I signed my receipt, took my bag, and I left.

I decided to go to where I was celebrated, and wouldn't just be around to be tolerated. I was going through my own problems, and I didn't need to be bothered with anyone's insecurities. Melanie was a great girl, but she said that she wanted to take things slow. I guess I was moving too slow for her now that she was ready to speed things up.

I hated that I went out of the city for this dinner. It took me almost thirty minutes to make it to Sin's condo.

I walked up to Sin's door with my to-go bag, and knocked hard on the door.

Sin answered the door wearing some leggings and a shirt.

"Don't you look comfy?" I walked past her.

"Yeah, because I'm in my condo with the heat on. What brought you by? And is this bag something for me?" I heard her lock the door.

I walked into the kitchen. There was an open bottle of wine sitting on the counter, which meant she was settling down for the evening. "I brought chicken alfredo and piece of salmon with fettuccine alfredo. Would you like some?"

"Of course." She walked to the cabinet and pulled out two plates.

I told her about my unfortunate date with Melanie while we ate. I didn't want to discuss too much of it with her, but it was nice to sit with her and talk with no judgement.

She caught me up on her last meeting with Heather-Nicole. I thought it was weird that Heather-Nicole wanted to meet with her so much, but I didn't speak on it. I was glad she was keeping me up to date on that situation, since I was the one who found out he was a married man. He was a disgrace, but I couldn't help but wonder what his motives were, too. Him reappearing as if he didn't have a family confused us both, but I told her not to stress herself out trying to figure it out. I thought it was funny that she nicknamed him "the great pretender". I thought it was perfect, because he was great at pretending.

"What are you thinking about doing?" I could see the wheels of Sin's brain spinning.

"Courtland, what are you talking about?" Sin was trying to act nonchalant, but I knew her too well.

"I know you're up to something." I watched her pour herself another glass of wine.

"No, I'm not." She rolled her eyes.

She was clearly lying, but I wasn't going to argue with her. She didn't have to tell me, as long as I knew that she was safe, I was fine with whatever she did.

I needed to tell her about Jackson's phone calls, but I decided against it because I didn't want to ruin our calm atmosphere. She didn't need to worry about anything that I wasn't one hundred percent sure about either. She had enough to deal with.

"What's going on with you? How's business?" She poured me another glass of Coke and Hennessey.

"Business is going well. How's everything with you, Dr. Beauty?"

Her face lit up, and I could feel myself slipping into her spell.

"You know what? Business is doing better than I expected. I've experienced some bumps along the way." Her face got really tense. "But I'm handling them the best way I know how. She gave me a reassuring smile, but I was still concerned.

"Really? What kind of bumps have you experienced?" I wanted to make sure she wasn't being hassled by Jackson too.

"Nothing worth talking about." She waved me off. "I'm still in the game."

"Yes you are." I kept my eyes on her. She looked beautiful sitting in her comfy lounge wear. Her hair was pulled back in a tight ponytail, showing all of the beautiful imperfections that made up her face. This woman was gorgeous, and I couldn't help but feel thankful to still be a part of her life.

"You're so sweet to me." She put her glass down on the end table closest to her, and took another bite of her alfredo.

"I try."

"So what's been going on? You've been quiet and distant, and you're neither of those things." She was trying to be funny.

"I can say the same for you."

"Oh, whatever." She dismissed my statement.

We both laughed and finished eating. I needed a good laugh after walking out on Melanie.

CHAPTER TWENTY-FIVE

Sinaiyah

I was excited about tonight. I had made up in my mind that tonight would be my last night with Landon. I had held on long enough, and couldn't do it anymore. I felt that I had him right where I needed him: trusting me, and expecting nothing but the best from me. I didn't want to handle this situation with pride but more like a responsible adult. I was too grown to be making vindictive decisions. I was ready to be upfront with him and let him know that I was aware of his wife. My soul was irritated from pretending like I didn't know the truth. I was barely sleeping at night and that wasn't acceptable.

The sun had already gone down and it felt really good outside. Fall was kicking in beautifully. I decided to pick him up from work and take him to dinner for his birthday.

I pulled up to his office, and took a quick look around my surroundings before heading inside. I hadn't been to his office before but it wasn't far from Atlanta. I didn't enjoy having to go backwards before I could go forwards, but I knew it would be worth it tonight.

I walked to the office door, and let myself in. "Hello?"

"Hey, Sinaiyah, give me one sec," he yelled from the back.

I didn't feel comfortable going to the back and had no desire to see his office. There was no telling what he was doing, and I felt safer by the door.

A moment later Landon came around the corner wearing a dark grey suit with purple accents.

"What a handsome birthday man you are." I was a sucker for a well-tailored suit. He looked like milk chocolate dipped in platinum.

Bitch focus, I had to remind myself.

"Thank you. You look beautiful, girl." He walked towards me and grabbed me by the hips. He kissed me like I was his woman, and I had to force myself to not enjoy it. I couldn't slip into his trance again.

"Where are you taking me tonight?"

"Can you just enjoy my surprise?" I leaned to the side and placed one hand on my hip.

"Whatever you say." He grabbed my hand and led me outside. He locked his office up and met me in my car.

I turned some jazz on so that we wouldn't ride in complete silence.

We pulled up to the valet and got out of the car.

"I don't believe I've been here."

"Let's say tonight is the night of firsts." He followed me inside. I made dinner reservations at the

Sun Dial restaurant for us. It was known as the spinning restaurant.

We made it to the top floor and were seated by the window. It was beautiful. I had never been here at night, but I did occasionally visit for business lunches.

"Baby, you really didn't have to do this." He looked unhappy, like he was ready to leave.

"What's wrong?"

"Nothing. I just don't want you to spend too much money on me. My birthday is just another day."

"Stop being modest. You deserve to be celebrated. Now let's live a little." I ordered us a bottle of wine so that he could stop bitching.

I didn't order anything special, just baked chicken. I wasn't in a mood to eat anything heavy. Landon on the other hand, decided on a steak, which was fine with me.

I kept the conversation as light as possible.

Landon started telling me a little bit more about what he was doing and why he came to Atlanta. I didn't listen completely. It no longer mattered, because I had no intentions of seeing him after tonight.

I made the decision to keep it classy for the rest of the evening and engage with him as if I cared. We continued to eat in peace as we looked at the beautiful view of Atlanta.

The valet brought my car around and I drove us to the hotel we would be staying at for the remainder of the evening.

A nervous rush of energy ran through me as we walked to our room. I was still gaining the strength I needed to let him know that we couldn't see each other.

"Sin, I really enjoyed myself tonight. Thank you." I could hear the sincerity in his voice. I wished he had told me about his wife and kids ahead of time. Maybe I wouldn't have hated him so much.

"Well, the night isn't over yet." I was standing between his legs, while he rubbed my hips up and down. I could see that he wanted me all over his face.

"It sure isn't." He had the biggest smile on his face. I remembered when his smile excited me, but I was truly over him. I didn't want anything else to do with him.

"That's good."

"So about this surprise you've gotten me all excited about."

"What about it?"

"Don't do me like that," he pouted. He pulled me down to him by my arms and kissed me, biting my bottom lip.

I removed his suit jacket and shirt and tie. "No need for all these clothes."

He took off his undershirt and unbuttoned his pants.

I took a step back from him. "Slow down. First, I need to slip into this." I went to my purse, pulled out a red satin lingerie set, and rubbed it across his face.

"Well, don't make me wait for long." He rubbed his hands together in anticipation.

"Wait!" I remembered. "I'm going to tie you up first."

"For what, Baby? I promise I'm not going anywhere." He leaned back on the bed.

"This is my assurance that you don't. Now, come here." I kissed him, crawled to the headboard, and laid back. I turned him to the side and handcuffed his hands to the decorative lamp on the nightstand.

"Damn, Baby." I crawled on top of him and covered his eyes with his tie.

"I don't want to spoil the surprise. You haven't seen me in anything like this before." I kissed him one more time and crawled from on top of him.

"I can't wait." His voice was sultry and deeper than usual.

I walked to the closet and Heather-Nicole came out of the closet. She gave me a satisfied look. When she called me back the other day, she was distraught. She told me that I was right and that she needed to do more than survive. I told her what I was planning, and she said that she would definitely be there when I broke things off with him.

"Alright, Landon Jones. You ready for me?" I tried to sound as seductive as I possibly could.

"Yeah, Baby." He had no clue what was about to happen.

Heather-Nicole took off his shoes and began massaging his feet. She had on a champagne colored lace dress. She crawled on top of his legs and began rubbing his dick through his pants.

"Oh, Baby." His breathing started speeding up and getting deeper.

"Quick question before we go any further." I was standing next to him by the nightstand.

"You could've already asked."

"Remember when you said you didn't have a wife?"

He frowned up his face, looking confused.

I took the tie off of his eyes. "So tell me who she is?"

Heather-Nicole was sitting on his lap with her arms folded across her chest. "Yeah, Landon. Who am I?"

Landon jumped, almost bringing down the lamp. He was trying to get from under Heather-Nicole, but she wasn't letting him up.

"No need to get hysterical." I placed my hand on his chest. "This beautiful woman wanted to join my celebration of you, and I felt it was rightfully so that she came, because she's your *wife*," I shouted.

He was so quiet. His eyes looked like they were about to pop out of their sockets.

"I don't understand why you would come back into my life when you have an obligation to your wife.

We've been through so much. I don't deserve your disrespect." I grabbed my purse from the bed.

"And neither do I." Heather-Nicole seemed really calm. I guess being in control made her feel like she was finally living.

"Alrighty then." I looked at him one last time. "I'll let you handle him however you choose." I looked through my purse and handed Heather-Nicole the keys to the handcuffs. "Personally, if I were you, I would leave the key on the bed, let him figure out how to free himself, and leave."

"Oh, I have an idea of what I'm going to do." Her tone was grim.

"Don't leave me here with her," he screamed.

I looked at him like I couldn't understand him.

"My Sin, please don't do this. You don't know who she really is."

"Shut-up, Landon!" Heather-Nicole finally spoke up for herself. "She knows exactly who you are."

"And I must say I'm not impressed."

"Don't believe anything she's told you. She's a manipulative, condescending woman."

"You really shouldn't talk about your wife that way. Remember you're tied up and she has the key." I gave him a sad face.

"We are not married! Please, Sin! Please!" I grabbed my purse, and turned my back to them. It didn't matter what he yelled out to me. He had lied long enough, and I didn't care to hear anything else. It didn't matter if they were married or not. The fact that he entered my life and brought her as baggage was enough.

"Enjoy." I gave her a wink, and headed to the door and didn't look back. I closed the door silently behind me, and headed to the stairwell. I ran down the steps to the next floor to catch the elevator. I needed to get out of that hotel and back to my condo immediately.

I couldn't believe I out pretended the great pretender. I felt accomplished and exhilarated. I felt free, as if a burden had been lifted off of me.

Fuck going home, I deserve a drink. The valet brought my car and I headed to a cute, little lounge. Tonight was my night to let loose.

CHAPTER TWENTY-SIX
Courtland

I was taking some time to myself today. Jazz played from my Bluetooth speakers, calming my spirit. I was comfortable walking around in my briefs with some socks on. It had been a long time since I enjoyed the comfort of my own home. Melanie had broken things off with me last week, and I wasn't expecting it. I knew I wasn't focused on our relationship like I should have been, but I had tried.

I was still deeply in love with Sin. I hated that I cared about her so much. I was ready for us to be back together, so that we could build our empire. We had wasted enough time. Sin was the girl that made me into a better man. I wasn't worried about women and their feelings. I had to be honest. I was selfish before I met her. I was used to having women; they were replaceable to me, but Sin wasn't.

My phone was vibrating on my kitchen counter, but I was in no mood to answer it. I wasn't sad or depressed. I just needed some time to myself. My business was doing just fine, and if anything was wrong I trusted that Damien could handle it.

I walked to the kitchen to pour a glass of Coke and Hennessey. I was content. I should have known that Melanie would break things off between us. She wasn't a dumb woman; she knew that Sin and I had business we needed to handle. Although, I still didn't regret my abrupt exit. I felt like I didn't have any energy to waste on faking a dinner. I didn't want her to stay, hopefully I made it easier for her too.

There was a knock on my door. I took my time walking to the door, because I wasn't expecting any company. I didn't want any shit to pop off either, and I wasn't ready. I was working on putting out positive energy.

I looked through the peephole and it was Sin. *See what positive thinking can do,* I thought to myself, as I quickly opened the door.

"What are you doing here?" I was really happy to see her.

"I have to make sure you aren't falling into a relationship breakup depression." She made her way into my condo.

"I wasn't in a relationship."

"Y'all still had a relationship, whether you all were exclusive or not." She laughed. "I just don't want you over here sad and hurting."

"Nobody is sad and hurting. I can assure you of that." Sin was so funny to me.

"Don't be mad that I'm doing a you, to you. You know how you were popping up on me, getting on my nerves like I wanted you around."

"You might not have wanted me around, but you needed me. I keep you grounded girl."

"And right now, you need me, so shut-up."

"Whatever you say."

"You're not even up and moving. Why?"

"Because I just woke up."

"Courtland. It's two in the afternoon, just an F.Y.I. You need to get moving."

"Have you been productive today?"

"Umm, yes!" She started laughing hard. "It's two in the afternoon. I'm actually done for today. Cynthia has the rest of the clients."

She was right. I needed to get up and start moving. "Since you're here," I walked up to her, and held her by the waist. "Let's not waste this time."

"I'm not giving you no sympathy sex." She tried to look at me with a straight face, but she couldn't help herself from laughing.

I wanted to tackle her for making a stupid joke. "You know what, let's go." I picked her up by her legs and took her to my bedroom. "Sympathy sex doesn't sound too bad." I threw her on the bed. "I'm already naked. Why aren't you?"

"Really, Courtland?" She covered her face with both of her hands.

"Don't act shy now. You had all the jokes a minute ago."

She sat up and took off her boots and her series of clothes. "

"My goodness, you are bundled." It felt like it was taking her forever to get undressed.

"I guess I'll make a stop by the office." I had missed six calls from Jenna. Damien hadn't called me so I knew whatever she needed wasn't that important.

"Okay." Sin was in the bathroom washing her hands. She had just finished fixing her hair.

"You coming with me?"

"I sure am." She responded with a big smile on her face. "You need the support. Remember?"

"Oh yeah. I forgot."

She walked out the bathroom looking very well put together. "I'm ready."

"Let me grab my purse."

We pulled up to the Palace about forty minutes later. Sin was craving a smoothie so we made a quick stop. I wasn't in any rush to get to the office, but I was trying to make sure I kept my positive energy flowing.

"You all are busy." Sin made an observation of how packed the parking lot was.

Seeing the Palace parking lot full of cars made me smile. It was nice to see my dream was still a dream and not a nightmare. Despite Jackson and his fake lawyers trying to pry into my company affairs, everything was perfect.

"Yeah. It's usually like this."

"Okay, big shit. I see you." She jumped out of my truck, with her smoothie in her hand.

We walked inside and my staff greeted us.

"Where are you going?" Sin was heading downstairs.

"Oh. I was thinking that I should get a massage real quick, and then meet you in your office."

"Let them know you're my guest. I'll have Jenna inform them as well." Her smile grew wider and she headed downstairs to the massage suite. It made me happy to see her happy. This may not have been our company the way I wanted it, but I enjoyed that she was comfortable enough to come in and go directly where she wanted to go.

"Hey!" Jenna ran up to me breaking my thoughts. "Where have you been? I've been calling you all day."

"Been busy. You need anything?" My irritation showed on my face. I hadn't even made it to my office before I was being approached.

"Umm, yes. A young lady has been waiting for you for the past four hours," she exaggerated the time, "and she won't leave until she speaks to you."

My irritation turned into a scowl. "Who is she?"

"Her name is Sakiya...Sika." She was struggling with the name. "I can't really remember how to pronounce it. She's a pretty, little Asian woman."

"Sakaë?" I asked.

"That's exactly it!" She snapped her fingers. "Anyway, she's here and she's been waiting for you. She says it's urgent but she won't tell me anything."

"Where is she?" I remembered meeting her at a bar from a few months ago. I was surprised that she knew where to find me.

"Sitting out back on the lanai." She began walking me to the back of the building.

"Okay, I got it from here."

I wasn't sure how Sakaë found me after the last time we saw each other. I didn't think she knew who I was. I headed outside to see if it was really the girl I fucked in a bar.

I stepped outside and walked towards her sitting in one of the oversized decorative chairs.

"Sakaë?" I waited for her to turn around. I felt I needed to brace myself. All of the positive energy I once had was gone from my body.

"Courtland?" She turned around and stood up from her seat.

My body flushed with anxiety when I looked at her. I hadn't seen this woman since our secret rendezvous. She looked exactly the same, this time she was smiling from ear to ear.

"What brought you into the Palace?"

"You." She rubbed her rounding belly. "You're going to be a father, and I figured it was time you knew."

"What?" I couldn't hide my rage. I was pissed off. I wasn't sure if she was playing a joke on me, but I was not fascinated by her presence or her claims to be carrying my child.

"I didn't want you to be upset." She looked down at her stomach, still caressing it. "I know it's been a minute since we last saw each other, but I wanted you to know that there was going to be a child in the world carrying your DNA."

I was stunned. I swallowed hard trying to calm myself. "How far along are you?"

"I'll be four months in two weeks. I'm due in March, and no, I do not know if I'm having a boy or girl just yet. We have a little time before finding that out. However, I did want to know if you would like to go to my doctor's appointment with me when that time comes."

"And you're absolutely sure I'm the father?" I was confused. This couldn't be happening to me.

"Yes. You're the only man I slept with around the end of June, my conception month."

"Wow." I was speechless. My world was starting to fall apart slowly. I already lost my girl, and now I had a baby one the way with a woman I had no intentions of ever seeing again.

My thoughts suddenly went to Sin. She was somewhere in my building enjoying herself. Things were going well between us, and I didn't need her to be upset with me right now. I couldn't let her know about this. I was having a problem accepting this for myself.

CHAPTER TWENTY-SEVEN

Sinaiyah

I was devastated listening to Courtland tell me about how a one-night stand ended up with a baby — his baby—on the way. My entire body went numb as he tried to explain the situation to me. I always saw myself having his first child. I always figured we would work through our mess and be with each other. I loved him so much, but I couldn't accept another woman's child. I felt bad for hoping that the child wasn't his, but he admitted to sleeping with her.

"I still don't know what to believe. We used a condom, and I don't remember it breaking." He sat in a chair across from me

"So if you used a condom and it didn't break, Courtland, how did she get pregnant?"

"I don't know." He shook his head from side to side.

He looked so distraught sitting at his desk. The thoughts in his head where flooding him, and I could see him drowning in them.

I tried to dismiss this in my mind because it wasn't my issue, but I loved him too much to not feel any hurt. One half of me felt like I couldn't be upset because we weren't together, but the other half of me felt betrayed. The only thing I was happy to know was that he used a condom while fucking that random bitch. I just hoped that he used a condom for all his hoes, because clearly he was fucking randoms.

"I need to go." I rose from my chair, but then I remembered that he drove. "Do you mind taking me back to my car?"

"Of course not." He stood up. "Please don't be upset. I have every intention of having a DNA test done when the baby gets here."

"I'm not mad, Courtland." I was trying to stay strong in front of him, but I was miserable on the inside.

Thank goodness he didn't live too far from his office. The car ride was uncomfortable for me. Courtland continued trying to explain himself. He was babbling. I could tell he was still in shock.

I pulled back up to my office at three-forty-five, and the office was clearing out. Jaslynn was still at the front desk, and Cynthia was in the back with one of her clients. I headed straight to my office, and I heard my phone ringing from my purse. I fished around looking for my phone. When I found it, I didn't recognize the number on my screen. It couldn't hurt to pick up, so I decided to pick up anyway.

"Hello. May I please speak to Ms. Sinaiyah Lockhart?"

"May I ask who's calling?"

"Yes. This is Agent Rachel Nelson with the Department of Internal Revenue. Is this a good time?"

"Oh, really? Yes, this is a great time to speak. I have been waiting for a phone call." I rushed back down the hall and motioned for Jaslynn to be quiet. She looked startled by me. I kept my finger in front of my lips so that she knew to stay silent, and I put my cellphone on speaker.

"Well, Agent Lang told me that there was a situation the last time she saw you. I apologize for responding so late, as I had other affairs to attend to. I reviewed her notes and it seems as though she wanted to do some fact checking."

I looked at Jaslynn, and she wasn't buying anything Agent Smith was saying.

"That's the thing. I'm not understanding what needs to be checked. I've only been in business for about four months, and you all have visited me twice already. I never received any emails or letters in the mail, someone just popped up."

"I do apologize for any inconvenience, but because you're local, it's sometimes easier to stop by."

"That doesn't make any sense to me. I still should have received a letter in the mail, or even a confirmation letter after Agent Lang's first visit."

"I can have one sent to you by the end of the week."

She didn't understand what I was saying. She had poor professional skills; both her and her employees.

Jaslynn looked at me. "Ask for a meeting," she mouthed to me.

"Okay. Well, since I work in Atlanta, and you all have a headquarters here, I'm going to stop by and have a meeting with you."

"Ma'am, you can't just stop by and meet with me. You have to have an appointment."

"But you can send your workers to my office without having an appointment with me." I wanted her to realize how dumb she sounded.

"Well, we're a government agency." She spoke matter-of-factly.

"Okay then, I'll be at your office in the next twenty minutes."

"That's unnecessary, Ms. Lockhart."

"No, it's not. I need to let your agent finish going through my tax information anyway. So my financial advisor and I will be there shortly."

"That's fine. Do you know where our office is located?"

"No, ma'am, but I have Google, so I'm sure I can find out."

"I'm on the fourth floor, in suite four-ten."

"Awesome. We'll be there shortly."

I stopped by Viviana's office to pick her up first. It was almost four o'clock, and the IRS closed at four-thirty. Viviana walked slowly out of her office. She turned around and locked the door. Her hips were spreading already; she was definitely carrying a boy.

I unlocked the doors so that she could get inside.

"Girl, so they finally called." She struggled getting in the car. She was breathing really hard.

"First of all, you're not even that big so why you breathing so hard."

She looked over at me and started laughing so hard she began to cry. "Shut-up!" She nudged me in my arm.

"But yeah, they finally called. Sorry to have to bring you out like this when your day was finally ending."

"Girl, no problem. You know I want to be there."

Viviana and I rode through Atlanta listening to the voice on my android give me directions. Viviana was laid back, resting her head on the headrest. She was exhausted and it showed. I hated to have her all over town, but it made me feel better that she wanted to come with me.

We pulled into the parking garage and headed to the elevator. Viviana pressed the button. The floor was practically empty. There was someone at the front desk, but no one else on the floor. The front desk-representative didn't even acknowledge us; she kept her eyes focused on the computer.

"Look. I know we have to go to suite four-ten." I grabbed Viviana's hand, she was still breathing hard.

I read the sign on the wall to figure out which way we needed to go. We walked up to the suite and knocked on the door.

I heard someone shuffling papers inside. The door opened and a really pretty Caucasian woman opened the door with a huge smile on her face. "You must be Ms. Lockhart."

"Are you Agent Nelson?"

"Yes, ma'am, I am. Why don't you come in so that we can finish our conversation?"

"Thank you." I tried to smile. Viviana, finally caught her breath and sat down beside me. There was a large round table with eight chairs.

Agent Smith took her seat, and continued looking through the papers that were spread in front of her. "I'm sorry, I'm trying to get these documents together. Agent Lang should be here momentarily." A smile never left her face.

My eyes narrowed. "So to finish our discussion from earlier, why haven't I received any written documents to correlate with all of these visits I've gotten from your workers?"

"I do apologize for any inconvenience we've caused you, and I hope that we can get this resolved as soon as possible."

Viviana gave me the same look of confusion I gave her. Agent Nelson hadn't answered my question, but tried to placate me. I wasn't sure if I wanted to be near her anymore. I turned back to her and she was deep into whatever the documents were in front of her.

"Do any of these papers pertain to me?" I reached for one of the documents, but she quickly pushed all the papers towards her. "Agent Nelson, if you aren't going to answer my questions, we can go, and I will figure out who I need to talk to. I'm sure what you and your agents have done to my company is illegal." I smiled at her and sat straight up in my chair.

She reached for the phone that was buzzing on the table. When she was done texting, she looked at me and smiled, which sent a nervous rush through my body.

"Okay, thank you for your time." I rose up from my seat and grabbed my purse.

"Ms. Lockhart, please take a seat so that I can assist you as best as I can."

"Girl, let's go." I looked down at Viviana, who was sitting up in her chair.

The door swung open, "Sinaiyah, darling!" I looked up quickly, because I knew the voice. In walked Victoria, with Agent Lang and a burly black man dressed in all black behind her.

"What in the hell?" My heart sank into my stomach. I took a step backwards and held my arm up in front of Viviana, trying to shield her. I didn't want her to get caught up in Victoria's foolishness. Victoria looked good in a red dress suit with a brown fur draped around her shoulders. She looked like she had just stepped out of a photo-shoot in Milan. Victoria looked like she had lost weight, but her skin was glowing and she looked happy. I wasn't sure how she was able to be so fabulous and not bring any attention to herself. The last I heard, there was a warrant out for her arrest, but that wasn't any of my business.

"Sinaiyah, darling. No need to fret, I'm only here to talk, and not for long, as I have somewhere I need to be."

"We have absolutely nothing to talk about." My heart was pounding in my chest. I hadn't planned on seeing Victoria, but I always imagined that I would give her the beating of a lifetime when I did. I tapped Viviana on the arm and motioned for her to get up. I wasn't sure if Victoria had anyone else with her; she was always full of surprises.

"Sinaiyah, I know we left off on a bad note, but I promise I only want to help."

"Help with what? There is nothing for you to help me with." I looked over at Agent Smith who had stepped to the back of the room behind Victoria. Agent Lang was standing beside her. I didn't know if they were real IRS workers or if they were just players in Victoria's scheme.

"Sinaiyah, dear, you need to let the past stay in the past, and let it go. Now, I'm only here to warn you."

240

I couldn't believe the words coming out of her mouth. I felt Viviana touch my lower back, which made me calm down. I didn't need to make this any more of a stressful environment for her.

"What the hell could you have to warn me about?" I placed my purse back on the table and put hands on my hips.

"I'm actually risking it all being here with you. I have nothing against you dear, but there are others who do."

"Who do you mean when you say others?" I didn't believe anything she was saying.

"Illeanna. Jackson. Those are just a few names of those who are mad that you got away with so much. Please be careful of those who you do business with. Not everyone wants you to succeed."

I was careful with who I had been doing business with. There weren't many in my circle and my life was going great.

"Excuse me? I didn't do anything, which is why I was able to move on with my life. And why should I trust you? You've hurt me more than anybody, which is why we're leaving." I didn't want to walk past her, because I didn't trust her. I didn't want to hear anything else she had to say. I knew the cards Victoria liked to play. She liked to play dirty and throw people under the bus at her own expense. If anyone was after me, it was her.

"You don't have to believe me. You'll see on your own soon enough. Just remember, I warned you first and you didn't believe me. Courtland is in trouble too. Don't be surprised if you hear from either one of them and they have demands. You can take that how you want, just know I've warned you."

"So how long will you be in town, Madam?"

"Wheels will be up in thirty for me." She threw her brown fur back over her arm and placed her all-black cat-eye shades back over her eyes. "I hope that you received the things that I've said to you today in the best way. Give my son my love for me. Ciao." She turned around and strutted out.

My thoughts were scrambled as I leaned my hands on the desk to catch my breath. This had to be a dream. I couldn't believe how calm I was able to stay in front of Victoria.

I looked down at Viviana and her eyes were wide open, looking as though she was holding back tears.

"Let's go, Viviana." I grabbed her arm, and she shot out of her chair. She didn't say anything. I could only imagine all of the thoughts going through her mind. "We're going to let them know what happened as soon as we get in the car." I was speaking of Courtland and Damien. I could see the worry showing all over her posture. Her eyes were still wide; she was still processing everything that happened.

We headed back to the car, and I helped Viviana get in on her side. I called Courtland as soon as I got the car. If he was in trouble, I had to let him know. I took a deep breath and waited for him to answer the phone.

"Hey, Courtland! Are you with Damien?" I jumped right into it.

"Yeah, we're at the office still. Are you okay?" His tone grew serious.

"No, and I have Viviana. We're on our way. Stay put," I shouted and hung up the phone. I sped through Atlanta, trying to get to them so that we could tell them what had just happed.

I replayed seeing Victoria and our conversation through my mind and my hands started trembling. I needed Courtland now, and I hated that I needed him.

Also Available from Shani Greene-Dowdell Presents

www.ingramcontent.com/pod-product-compliance
Lightning Source LLC
Chambersburg PA
CBHW071145170626
46809CB00002B/785